P9-CFU-985

As
Dea
blo

This time the costumed Deathstalker didn't fight back. She staggered backward with a shriek.

"Hey!" she cried, grabbing her arm. "I'm bleed-ing!"

For a second I thought this was all part of the game. Then I remembered. In the comics, Deathstalker bleeds bluish green—like those scars on her body. And the substance I could already see seeping out from beneath the girl's hand was red.

Blood red.

THE HARDY BOYS

Undercover Brothers®

Available from Simon & Schuster

THE HARDY BOYS
Undercover Brothers

FRANKLIN W. DIXON

#37 Movie Menace

BOOK ONE IN THE DEATHSTALKER TRILOGY

Aladdin

New York   London   Toronto   Sydney

ALADDIN
An imprint of Simon & Schuster Children's Publishing Division
1230 Avenue of the Americas, New York, NY 10020
First Aladdin paperback edition May 2011
Copyright © 2011 by Simon & Schuster, Inc.
All rights reserved, including the right of reproduction
in whole or in part in any form.
ALADDIN is a trademark of Simon & Schuster, Inc., and related logo is a registered trademark of Simon & Schuster, Inc.
THE HARDY BOYS MYSTERY STORIES is a trademark of
Simon & Schuster, Inc.
HARDY BOYS UNDERCOVER BROTHERS and related logo are registered trademarks of Simon & Schuster, Inc.
For information about special discounts for bulk purchases, please contact Simon & Schuster Special Sales at 1-866-506-1949 or
business@simonandschuster.com.
The Simon & Schuster Speakers Bureau can bring authors to your live event. For more information or to book an event contact the
Simon & Schuster Speakers Bureau at 1-866-248-3049 or visit our website at www.simonspeakers.com.
Designed by Karina Granda
The text of this book was set in Aldine 401 BT.
Manufactured in the United States of America 0611 OFF
10 9 8 7 6 5 4 3 2
Library of Congress Control Number 2010939281
ISBN 978-1-4424-0258-4
ISBN 978-1-4424-0259-1 (eBook)

TABLE OF CONTENTS

JOE

Speedy Delivery

"**H**old on!" I shouted at my brother.

I hauled the wheel around. The sleek little motorboat skidded into the turn, its hull bouncing against the choppy, windswept water of the Chesapeake Bay.

The boat we were chasing was now racing straight toward the wooded shoreline. For one crazy second I thought the driver might keep going and ram the hull right up onto the rocky beach.

Then, with seconds to spare, he pulled it around to the left. The boat skimmed along the swells, running parallel to the shore.

"Whoa!" my brother Frank yelled. He clung to the side of our boat. "The water's way too shallow there! Turn now, Joe. We'll have to wait for them to come back out here."

He was right. Frank usually is. He's a smart guy; everyone says so.

But I wasn't about to let these lowlifes jump out and swim to shore. They'd disappear into the woods before I could get our boat turned around.

"No choice, bro," I called over the whine of the motor. "I'm going in."

Frank yelled something else. I didn't hear him. For one thing, the motor got even louder as I eased it into another turn. For another, I was totally focused on that other boat.

There were two guys in it. One was bent over the wheel. The other glanced back at us.

He looked angry. Teenage drug runners usually do when they know they're about to get caught.

I let the motor out another notch.

"This is crazy!" Frank's voice broke through my focus. He sounded freaked out. Nerdy older brothers usually do when their studly, fearless younger brothers are doing something gutsy. "If they don't get in deeper water stat, they're going to—"

CRASH!

The noise hit me first. The sight seemed to happen in slow motion.

I saw the boat ahead of us stop short.

No, not quite stop.

It sort of crumpled, then the stern of the boat flew upward. It flipped over in midair . . .

SPLASH!

My slow-motion vision ended as the overturned boat hit the water. I heard Frank yelling again, but I ignored him. I was busy hauling the wheel to the left, trying to turn our boat before we smashed into the wreck.

"Too late!" I yelled, realizing there was nothing I could do. Not unless I suddenly figured out a way to beat the laws of physics.

I let go of the wheel and dove for the edge of the boat. I could only hope that Frank caught on and followed. Like I said, he's a smart guy. But sometimes he's too cautious, a little too slow to act. . . .

"Jump!" I cried as I flung myself over the boat's edge.

Oof. I belly flopped into the water. The wake of our speeding boat spun me around like a washing machine beating up on a pair of dirty socks. I wasn't sure which way was up.

Even though I was still underwater, I felt the shudder as our boat hit the wreckage.

KABOOM!

The water rippled with the force of the explosion, sending me on a few more rotations.

I fought my way to the surface, squinting to get the murky water out of my eyes. Frank. Where was Frank? Had he made it off the boat in time?

"I told you not to get so close to shore," a familiar voice said from a few feet behind me.

Whew! I'd never been so glad to hear one of Frank's I-told-you-so's.

"What happened to those guys?" I asked, treading water as I tried to get my bearings. "Think they survived that smashup?"

"Probably." Frank peered at the floating, smoking wreckage. "Their boat just hit some rocks. Nothing exploded until ours crashed into theirs. They're probably still trying to get away."

Frank knew we weren't exactly dealing with a couple of geniuses. After all, geniuses wouldn't be making their living smuggling drugs and selling them to little kids.

"Let's go find them." I struck out for the wreckage.

I'd only swum a few yards when I saw one of the non-geniuses. He was clinging to a piece of hull. His buddy was treading water nearby.

Frank saw them too. "Stop right there!" he yelled.

The geniuses ignored him and took off toward shore. No big surprise there. Criminals hardly ever obey when you yell at them to "stop right there." At least not in my experience. And I have plenty. After all, Frank and I have been ATAC agents since our dad started the agency.

But more on that later.

"I'll get the ugly one!" I yelled. "You grab Mr. Hair Gel."

I dove under and kicked forward, aiming at one of the drug runners. *Oof!* One of his feet clocked me in the side of the head. Yeah, that was going to leave a bruise.

He kicked his feet harder as he swam away faster. Or tried to, anyway. I grabbed one of his ankles and held on tight. When my head popped out of the water, I heard the guy cursing and sputtering.

"Got him!" I yelled to Frank.

Frank didn't answer. I looked over and saw him struggling with the other guy. Frank was trying to get him in a hammerlock, but the guy kept landing punches. They weren't very hard ones, but still.

"Hey!" I blurted out as I felt my guy wriggle loose. He yanked his foot away and kicked me in the thigh, then took off. Who knew drug runners were such fast swimmers?

"Get him!" Frank yelled. Then he gurgled. Uh-oh. His guy had just dunked both of their heads underwater.

Time for a new plan. I had to think fast.

"Whoa!" I yelled as loudly as I could. "Watch out for that shark!"

Okay, it was kind of a lame plan. But it was all I had at the moment.

And it worked. Frank's guy stopped fighting and looked around goggle-eyed. That gave Frank the chance to get him in that hammerlock.

My guy started spinning around in a panic, looking for the shark. Two quick strokes and I was on him.

"Let me go!" the guy yelped. "The shark'll get us both!"

"Yeah," I muttered as I struck off toward shore, yanking the guy behind me. "Real geniuses."

"That might be a record," Frank said as he rubbed his damp hair with a towel. "I don't think we've ever completed a mission in a day and a half before."

I was sprawled on one of the hotel room's double beds. It was a pretty nice room. Too bad we'd only had one night to enjoy it.

"Yeah. Maybe we should spend a few days at

the beach somewhere down the coast," I said, only half joking. Okay, I admit it, maybe not even half. "I mean, why not? Mom and Aunt Trudy think this Young Diplomats Conference we're supposed to be attending lasts almost two more weeks."

"Somehow I don't think ATAC's going to go for that," Frank said.

Yeah. I didn't think so either.

In case you're wondering, ATAC stands for American Teens Against Crime. My dad, Fenton Hardy, started the supersecret agency a few years back. Dad's a retired PI who did a lot of under-cover work in his day, and he realized there were times when an adult agent couldn't blend in. Like at a BMX rally. In a mosh pit. At a high school prom. Places like that.

But a teenage undercover agent? Piece of cake!

And so ATAC was born. Frank and I were the first two teens to sign up. We've been fighting crime ever since.

Dad knows all about it, of course. Mom and Aunt Trudy? Not so much. It can be tough com-ing up with cover stories every time we take off on a mission. This time it was a fictional Young Diplomats Conference in Washington, D.C. What were we supposed to tell everyone when we returned home after two days instead of two weeks? That we weren't diplomatic enough? They might believe I'd gotten myself kicked out. But not my brother, Mr. Straight-A-Eagle-Scout.

Really, that beach thing was sounding like more of a plan all the time. All we'd be left to explain was our tans. And didn't we deserve a little R & R after solving the case so fast?

I rolled over and sat up. "We didn't even get the chance to use our latest gizmo," I said, lifting my hand. One of the cool things about working for ATAC is the gadgets. This time Frank and I had each gotten rings. Okay, that doesn't *sound* very cool. But it was. These looked like ordinary class rings, the kind tons of high schoolers and college students wear. But they each contained a tiny, sophisticated GPS-type device. If Frank and I got separated, we'd be able to use the rings to track and find each other. Pretty important when you work as a team.

Frank glanced at his ring and shrugged. "Yeah. Maybe next mission."

Just then there was a knock at the door. "Room service!" a muffled voice called from the hallway.

"We didn't order anything," Frank said. Then he shot me a suspicious look. "Did we?"

"No," I replied. "But that's not a bad idea. I wonder if they have pizza."

Frank was already hurrying toward the door. He swung it open. "Thanks," he began. "But we didn't . . ."

His voice trailed off. There was nobody there. But a tray topped by a silver dome had been left sitting in the hall.

"Weird," I said. "Think it's a bomb?"

I was kidding. At least I hoped so. Sometimes being an ATAC agent gives you a warped sense of humor.

"They must have dropped this food off at the wrong room," Frank said.

"Yeah." I pushed past him and grabbed the tray. "Let's see what it is before we decide if we should return it. All that swimming made me hungry."

I set the tray on a table and pulled off the domed cover. There were no burgers on the plate. No pizza. Not even a bologna sandwich. No bomb, either.

There was just a thin silver disk.

"Whoa," Frank said. "Looks like we don't have time to hit the beach after all. I think we just got our next mission!"

Comic Relief

"Pop it in, bro!" Joe urged as I picked up the disk.

"Okay." I grabbed my suitcase and pulled out our portable DVD player. We almost always keep it with us, mostly for times like this. ATAC HQ always sends our mission instructions on disks. They look like ordinary CDs or DVDs, but we know better.

I set up the machine, stuck in the disk, and pressed play.

First our ATAC boss, known only as Q, appeared and greeted us. Then his face faded and a logo popped up on-screen: a glowing golden yellow scorpion. It looked kind of familiar.

"Whoa!" Joe exclaimed. "Deathstalker!"

Oh, right. Now I recognized the scorpion logo. Deathstalker is the title character in a series of popular comic books. She's a teenage girl with superpowers, including the ability to sting like a scorpion.

That was about all I knew. I pretty much stopped reading comics when I was ten.

But not my brother. He's still into them. And he calls *me* a nerd?

There was no time to harass him about that just then, though. Our mission disks only play once, then they self-destruct. See, that's not something that just happens in the movies. They don't actually blow up or anything, but the messages are set to erase after a single viewing. If anyone tries to play the disk after that, all they'll see is a music video or something.

Joe tends to get excited and forget that sometimes. More than once, we've almost missed our instructions.

"Focus," I told him, my finger poised over the pause button just in case.

He settled down, his eyes glued to the screen. The scorpion logo exploded, shrapnel flying in all directions. Then a pretty, dark-haired girl appeared. She was dressed in black leather from head to toe. The same scorpion was emblazoned on her chest. She stood there for a second, then spun around and raced away.

"Wait, I've seen this!" Joe exclaimed.

"What?" I hit pause. "What do you mean you've seen it?"

"It's an early trailer." Joe waved his hand. "You know, like a preview for the *Deathstalker* movie. It's been all over the Internet for the past week or two."

"They're making a movie out of the comic books?"

Joe rolled his eyes. "*All* the great comics get turned into movies—usually awesome ones."

"If you say so." I hit play and the trailer continued. More explosions. More of the pretty girl in the tight leather jumpsuit. Lots of action and running around. It was hard to tell what the plot was supposed to be, but maybe that wasn't important.

Finally the picture froze on a close-up image of the girl's face, and Q's voice came on in voice-over.

"You're being called to New York City to pose as extras on a movie set," Q said. "The movie is a big-budget adaptation of the popular superhero comic Deathstalker."

"Like, duh!" Joe broke in.

"Starring as the title character is a teenage girl named Anya Archer. She was plucked from obscurity after an intense nationwide talent search."

"Oh yeah, I heard about that," Joe commented. "It was on all the entertainment blogs awhile back. Practically every actress in Hollywood wanted the role, but the director insisted he wanted an unknown."

Naturally, I'd already hit pause again. "Interesting," I said. "Mission on a movie set, huh? Sounds pretty cool."

"Not just any movie set!" Joe's eyes were gleaming. "The set of *Deathstalker*! Oh man—the only bad part is that I won't be allowed to tell anyone about this!"

That was part of the ATAC deal. The only way we can pull off our missions is by staying undercover. That means nobody is supposed to know what we do. Most people don't even know ATAC exists. That includes Mom, Aunt Trudy, and all our friends back home.

"That's okay," I told Joe with a slight smirk. "If you told anyone, you'd also have to admit that you still read comic books."

Joe barely seemed to hear me. "I wonder what the mission is."

"One way to find out." I hit play again.

Q came back on-screen. "ATAC has been called in because of a few mysterious problems on the set, most notably a fire. Anya believes she's being targeted—that someone is out to get her. Your job is to find out whether she's right before anyone gets hurt. Since the cast is mostly teenagers, it should be easy for you to blend in as extras on the film. The only people who will know your true identities are Anya and the film's director, Jaan St. John."

"Whoa!" I paused the recording again. "Did he just say Jaan St. John is directing this thing?"

Joe shrugged. "Yeah, so what? He's just some director, right?"

"Just some director?" It was my turn to roll my eyes. "I guess I should expect that from a guy who thinks superhero comics are great literature. Jaan St. John won just about every serious film award last year for his independent film *Milady*."

"*Milady*?" Joe looked dubious. "Never heard of it."

"I'm not surprised. There's not a single explosion in it. It's a docudrama that draws parallels between the life cycle of ladybugs and the life of Mary, Queen of Scots."

"Sounds like a thrill a minute." Joe was back to rolling his eyes. "Anyway, now that you mention it,

I remember reading about him on those entertainment blogs too. I guess he's supposed to be some kind of kooky-artsy creative genius or something. Don't ask me why they'd hire him to direct something like *Deathstalker*."

"They're probably trying to class it up. But forget that—the mission sounds a little vague so far. Let's find out the other details."

I turned the disk back on. But there weren't many other details. Just the usual info about how to get where we were going and such.

"Oh well," I said as the recording ended. "Guess we'll find out more when we get to New York."

"Yeah," Joe said. "And I guess the beach will have to wait."

"This is awesome!" Joe said.

It was seven o'clock the next morning. Joe and I had arrived in New York City the night before, checked into our hotel, and fallen into bed. Now we were on location at the movie set waiting to meet with the director, Jaan St. John.

Joe looked pretty happy, especially considering the early hour. But I understood why. The movie set was a pretty cool place.

From the outside, it hadn't looked like much— just a bunch of trailers and sheds lined up behind temporary fencing on the Great Lawn in Central Park. A guard had stopped us at the gate, but a quick call to Jaan St. John had gotten us in.

Now we could see that the place was all hustle and bustle. Burly men wheeled huge cameras here and there. People with clipboards raced around, barking orders into cell phones. Workers were setting up a bunch of scaffolding and scenery nearby.

"I bet I know what scenes they're shooting here," Joe said eagerly. "It's probably the part when Deathstalker first faces off against the evil aliens and discovers more of her powers."

"Hold on," I said. "Aliens?"

Joe looked at me as if *I* was an alien. "Duh," he said. "Are you so busy watching movies about ladybugs that you've never even read the first page of a Deathstalker comic?"

I shrugged. "So sue me. I have taste."

"If you say so." Joe snorted. "But listen, bro, this is part of our mission. You really need to get up to speed. See, Deathstalker started life as ordinary suburban teen Sissy Stiles. Then one day an alien spaceship crashed into her house, killing the rest of her family and leaving her in a coma. The only reason she survived at all is because Sissy's best friend, Susie Q, risked her own life to pull Sissy out of the flames."

"Susie Q?" I said. "Really?"

"Hey, I didn't make up the names," Joe said. "Anyway, when Sissy wakes up from the coma, she finds out that the brilliant but psycho surgeon Dr. Ezekiel Brayne has used a risky and totally untested medical procedure to revive her. He injected her with a serum made from the deadly deathstalker scorpion's venom."

"That's actually a real kind of scorpion," I commented. "They're found in Northern Africa and the Middle East."

"Thanks, Mr. Wikipedia," Joe said, making a face.

"Hey, you should know that too, Mr. Short Attention Span," I countered. "We learned about them in that ATAC training seminar on neurotoxins, remember?"

"Sure, whatever. Anyway, Sissy ends up changing her name to Deathstalker because of that and also because one of her powers is being able to immobilize her enemies by digging her long fingernails into their skin and poisoning them with the toxic scorpion venom in her blood."

"Okay, I'm no doctor, but I seriously doubt the venom would stay in her blood like that." I had to step back as a harried-looking woman rushed past, carrying a bunch of extension cords. "Plus, even if it did, how would it get into her fingernails from there?"

Joe looked annoyed. "This isn't science class, okay? It's a superhero comic. Deal with it."

"I could deal with it better if it bore any passing resemblance to scientific accuracy," I said. "But never mind. Anything else I should know?"

"Well, the burns from the alien crash site leave weird blue and green scars all over her body, which is why she wears that hot leather jumpsuit," Joe said, leaning against a huge piece of camera equipment. "When Sissy—now Deathstalker—returns to the scene of the accident, she finds this creepy-looking eight-foot-tall alien named Asp huddled in the ashes. He's the only survivor from the alien ship. She starts to sting him, but he stops her by telling her that his ship crashed because it was shot down by some evil aliens who are trying to take over Earth. So the two of them, plus Susie Q, team up to try to track down and destroy the evil aliens and also end up righting other wrongs and stuff along the way. But they have to keep dodging Dr. Brayne, who wants to find Deathstalker so he can lock her up in his lab and study her like a lab rat."

"Wow. That's quite a story." Now I understood why the movie trailer on our DVD hadn't made any sense to me.

Before I could say anything else, I saw someone heading toward us. It was a tall, blond dude around our age or maybe a little older. You know how certain people get described as having "movie-star good looks"? Well, that was this guy. White teeth, square jaw, broad shoulders, the works.

"Excuse me," he said, sounding kind of suspicious. "I haven't seen you two around here. This is a closed set, you know. Do you have ID?"

As a matter of fact, we did. A packet had been waiting for us at our hotel last night, complete with fake driver's licenses sporting our names for this mission: Frank Miller and Joe Clark.

"Sure," Joe began. "We're—"

"Hello, hello!" a new voice broke in. A second later a man hurried over. He was about fifty years old, had a beard, and was kind of short. His twinkling blue eyes held a hint of mischief.

Even dressed in khaki shorts and high-top sneakers instead of a tux, I recognized him right away from the awards show clips I'd seen on TV: Jaan St. John.

"Don't fret, Vance," the director told the blond guy. His voice had a light European accent, though I couldn't quite place it. "These boys aren't here to cause mischief and mayhem. I was just looking for them, in fact."

"Oh, okay." The blond guy—Vance—looked a little less aggressive. "I was just checking. After the fire and everything, you never know. . . ."

"Fine, fine." St. John beamed at him, then turned to us. "Vance is one of our actors. Now come along, my children. We'll talk in my office."

His office turned out to be in one of the trailers parked nearby. The interior was pretty wild. Parts of it looked like a normal office, like the desk and the filing cabinet and the laptop computer.

But most of the offices I've seen don't have an Australian didgeridoo leaning in the corner. Or a framed display of huge, weird-looking insects pinned to a velvet backing. Or what looked an awful lot like a genuine shrunken head hanging from the ceiling fan.

"Whoa." Joe stared at something in a glass case atop the filing cabinet. "Is that a real elephant tusk?"

"Yes, it was given to me by a friend on my first visit to the Dark Continent many moons ago," St. John said with a cheerful smile. "Quite illegal to procure such things now, of course. But please— make yourselves comfortable."

I wasn't sure how that was going to be possible, given the toothy mounted crocodile head glaring at us from one wall. But Joe and I sat down in the guest chairs in front of the desk while the director settled himself behind it.

"Now," he said. "Shall we discuss the reasons for your visit to our humble workspace?"

"Sure," Joe said. "I—"

The rest of his words were lost in an ear-shattering explosion from somewhere just outside.

3

JOE

Blastoff

Frank and I were on our feet instantly. "Dude, what was that?" I cried.

Without waiting for an answer, I raced for the door. Frank was at my heels.

"Wait, boys!" Jaan called. "It's not—"

I didn't hear any more. I shoved open the trailer door and leaped to the ground, bypassing the steps.

"Over there!" Frank shouted, landing beside me.

I looked where he was pointing. Black smoke was pouring out of a metal barrel about a hundred feet away.

"Stop!" Jaan appeared in the doorway behind us. "It's only Scorch testing the explosives for a scene we're shooting later."

"Huh?" I said.

Yeah, I'm not real articulate when I think I'm about to get blown up.

Jaan pointed to a wild-haired man leaning over the barrel. "That's Scorch. He's our special effects man. Best in the business." He leaned closer and winked. "Even if some people think he's a bit crazy."

After seeing his Wild Kingdom of an office, I was already thinking this guy wasn't one to talk.

But I forgot about that as one of the most gorgeous girls I'd ever seen in real life emerged from the next trailer. Okay, Frank would probably tell you that I think *every* girl is the most gorgeous girl I've ever seen. But this time it was no exaggeration. I knew immediately that she had to be an actress. Judging by her wholesome blond looks, I figured she was probably playing Susie Q.

"Jaan!" she exclaimed. Even her pout was pretty. "Can't you tell Scorch to warn people when he's going to do that? Lila almost drew another mouth on my face while she was trying to put on my lip liner!"

"Apologies, Harmony, my child," Jaan said with a little bow. "I'll speak to Scorch, but you know how he is. Everything fades away to unimportance when he's bringing one of his babies to fiery life."

He smiled. "Besides, if you're to be an action star, you'll have to get used to such things. This isn't your talky, broody TV show where nothing louder than a tragic breakup ever happens."

"Tragic breakup?" I echoed, confused.

"Ah, but don't you recognize our lovely young star, Joe?" Jaan turned to smile at me. "This is Harmony Caldwell, the former star of *Young Hearts*."

Okay, now I knew who she was. *Young Hearts* was a huge hit—a teen TV drama set at an exclusive private high school. Not that I ever watched it myself. Angst and gooey romance aren't really my things. But Aunt Trudy, who lives with us, never missed an episode.

Now, looking at Harmony, I was wondering if I should've been watching after all.

"Nice to meet you," I told Harmony with my most charming smile. "I'm a big fan."

Frank shot me a look, but I ignored him. Meanwhile Jaan checked his watch.

"Have you seen Anya, my dear?" he asked Harmony.

"I think she's in her trailer," Harmony replied.

Jaan thanked her and glanced at us. "Come," he said. "You've met our established young actress. Now let me introduce you to our rising star."

As Harmony went back to finish up her makeup,

the director led us to another trailer. He barely had time to knock before the door swung open.

"Are they here?" the girl inside demanded. Her ice blue eyes swept over Frank and me. "Oh, good!"

"I told you I'd take care of things, Anya my dear," Jaan said calmly. "Shall we all sit down and get acquainted?"

The girl nodded and let us into the trailer. It was basically one big open room. At one end was a makeup counter and mirror; at the other was a small kitchenette. The rest of the space was a sitting area with cushy sofas and stuff.

Not that I was paying much attention to the furniture. I was way more interested in checking out Anya.

I could definitely see why she'd been cast as Deathstalker. She looked exactly like the comic character. I mean *exactly*. Lush dark wavy hair tumbling over her shoulders. Those amazing blue eyes. Legs a mile long. She even had Deathstalker's trademark slight gap between her two front teeth.

Not that I got a very good look at her teeth. Anya wasn't smiling much. She looked kind of tense, actually.

"So you two are really professionals?" she asked, sounding a little dubious.

Jaan chuckled. "I'm told these lads are two of ATAC's most accomplished and capable young agents," he assured her. "They'll get to the bottom of things—no need to fret. You can relax now and focus on becoming your character. All right, my child?"

Anya nodded. "Okay," she said in a small voice. But her eyes were troubled.

"Good." Jaan clapped his hands. "So shall we discuss the strange goings-on around the set lately? Get you boys up to speed so you can start solving all our problems?"

"Sure," Frank said. "By the way, just to confirm—you two are the only ones who know our real identities, right?"

Jaan nodded. "That's right. We haven't told anyone else, not even my assistant director or Anya's agent."

"Not that he'd care." Anya rolled her eyes. "He's off in L.A., perfecting his fake tan to get ready for the Big Apple Awards."

Coming from most people, a comment like that might sound kind of obnoxious. But from Anya, it just sounded a little sad. It made me want to hug her. Okay, her gorgeous face and hot body already made me want to hug her. But that, too.

"Should we begin by telling our intrepid young agents about the fire?" Jaan asked.

"I guess." Anya glanced at him. "By the way, Big Bobby just texted me. He's running late. Again."

"Big Bobby?" I asked.

"Her primary bodyguard," Jaan explained. Then he turned to Anya. "I'm sorry to hear that, my dear. But I can assure you, Big Bobby came highly recommended by several of my fellow directors. He'll keep you safe, not to worry."

"How can he keep me safe when he's not even here half the time?" Anya bit her lip. "Actually, I have an idea. Since there are two ATAC agents, maybe one of them should be like an additional bodyguard. You know—stick close to me in case anything else happens."

"I'm not sure that will work," Frank spoke up. "Our cover story is supposed to be that we're extras."

"That's exactly what I need. An extra bodyguard." Anya finally cracked a smile, though only for a second. Then she turned to Jaan. "Please? I'd feel a lot better if I knew I had someone reliable protecting me all the time."

The director shrugged. "You know I cannot resist a sincere plea from a pretty face," he said, tickling Anya under the chin as if she were an oversize baby. "Let it be done!"

Frank and I traded a look. I could tell what

he was thinking. Posing as extras was the perfect cover—we'd be able to wander around together or separately anywhere on set without raising suspicion. It would be a lot harder if one of us was stuck shadowing Anya.

Then again, I was ready to embrace the silver lining. Shadowing Anya didn't sound like the worst job in the world. She was hot, she was about to be famous, and so far she seemed pretty cool.

I was about to open my mouth to volunteer when Jaan pointed at Frank. "You," he said. "You'll stay with Anya. But we won't call you a bodyguard, all right? No need to arouse suspicion or envy by giving her another personal bodyguard. You can pose as her boyfriend, freshly arrived from back home in Apple Valley, Minnesota."

"Wait, are you sure?" I blurted out. "Maybe we should really think about which of us will be more convincing as her boyfriend. . . ."

"It is already decided," Jaan announced. "Frank is taller and more handsome than you are, thus better suited for the part."

I scowled. Taller, okay, I could give him that. But Jaan had to be half-blind if he seriously thought nerdy Frank was more handsome than me!

But I figured it wouldn't do much good to

grumble about it. This guy was a director—he was used to calling the shots.

Besides, I'd just gotten a look at Frank's face. He'd smirked for a second at Jaan's comment, then started to look nervous.

I could pretty much read his mind. Frank isn't exactly Mr. Suave when it comes to the ladies. He gets tongue-tied trying to talk to the cute check-out girl at the supermarket back home in Bayport. How was he going to handle acting as the love interest of a gorgeous soon-to-be movie star? I wasn't sure, but it was probably going to be amusing to watch.

So there. I had my silver lining after all.

Just then there was a knock at the door. It swung open, and a sixtyish man with droopy jowls stuck his head in.

"There you are, Jaan," he said in a gravelly voice. "I've been looking all over for you. Don't you ever answer your phone?"

"Only when I feel like it," Jaan answered calmly. "What can I do for you, Stan?"

"We need to talk about the budget," the man said. If he'd noticed there were other people in the room, he gave no indication of it. "I really wish you'd run some of your ideas by me before you implement them. That wind tunnel contraption you rented is costing a fortune, and if you're serious about adding the scene where Brayne crashes a city bus into the Hudson River . . ."

"All right, all right. We shall talk." Jaan stood and glanced at us. "You young people can continue this party without me, hmm?" Not waiting for an answer, he hurried out after the other man.

"Who was that?" Frank asked when they were gone.

"Stan Redmond," Anya said. "He's the producer of this film. He's like the money guy, I guess—at least he's always complaining about how much all Jaan's wacky new ideas cost."

"So this is really your first movie role ever, huh?" I asked.

"Uh-huh." She smiled sheepishly. "First acting job ever, actually. It's a little crazy. I only went to the audition because my friends talked me into it. They're convinced that I look just like Deathstalker."

"You totally do," I said.

"That's what Jaan said as soon as he saw me. Before I knew what was happening, here I was! Anyway, thanks for coming. I feel a little better just knowing someone's taking the problems seriously."

"Exactly what problems?" Frank asked. "ATAC

didn't give us many details. They just said something about a fire. . . ."

"Yeah." Anya glanced around her trailer. "My first dressing room burned down last week. Like, ten minutes after I left to get coffee with Harmony. It's lucky I wasn't inside taking a nap!"

"Really?" I leaned forward. "Arson?"

"I don't know." Anya shrugged and sighed. "The fire department and police came to investigate, but Jaan won't give me a straight answer about what they found."

"Yeah, I believe it," I said. "I just met the guy, but he kind of talks in circles."

Anya laughed. "That's just Jaan," she said. "He's pretty cool, actually. He's been super supportive of me, even though I have so much to learn about this whole acting thing. Sometimes I feel like he's the only one who—"

At that moment the door flew open and a woman burst in. She was about the age of my grandma, with little half-moon glasses perched on her nose and gray hair pulled into a tight bun.

"Oh! So sorry, sweetie," she cooed. "I didn't realize you had company." She peered at Frank and me with curious hazel eyes. "Who have we here?"

I gulped. Great. We'd only been here about five seconds, and already our cover was looking shaky.

How were we going to explain why some random extra was hanging out with Anya and her boyfriend?

But being an ATAC agent is all about being quick on your feet. Frank was already speaking up to introduce himself as "Frank Miller of Apple Valley, Minnesota."

"Yes. Frank and I have been dating since, like, eighth grade," Anya added. Leaning closer to Frank, she hugged his arm and gave him a dazzling smile. "I missed him so much that I finally talked him into flying out to visit for a while."

Wow. This might be her first acting job, but she was pretty convincing. Frank actually looked a little overwhelmed.

But he plowed on, introducing me by my cover name. "Joe's an old buddy of mine from back home," he improvised. "We went to summer camp together. He's always wanted to be an actor, so Anya helped him get a gig as an extra on this film. We both flew in this morning from Apple Valley."

Good old Frank! He might be hopeless with girls, but the guy can think fast. It was the perfect cover story. Now we could talk to each other as much as we wanted without raising suspicion.

"How nice." The woman clasped her hands. "And how lovely that you came to see Anya, Frank.

You two must miss each other dreadfully being so far apart. . . ."

I didn't hear the rest of what she said. I'd just heard a soft buzz from nearby. I glanced over just in time to see Anya look down at her cell phone. All the color suddenly drained out of her face as she stared at the tiny screen.

Uh-oh. That couldn't be good.

"Anyway, we just arrived and were catching up," I said loudly, hoping the woman—whoever she was—would take the hint.

Luckily, she did. "How nice. I'll leave you to it, then. I'm sure Anya is eager for all the news from home." She beamed at me. "If you see Harmony around anywhere, would you be a dear and let her know that Vivian's looking for her?"

"Sure." Frank stood up politely and held the door as the woman left.

"What?" I asked Anya as soon as the door shut behind the woman.

Wordlessly, Anya held up her phone. Frank and I leaned closer to see the text message on the screen. It was short and not so sweet.

U WILL NEVER LIVE 2B DEATHSTALKER!

FRANK

4

A Sudden Change in Plans

"Who sent this?" Joe grabbed the phone out of Anya's hand.

"I don't know," she said, her voice shaking. "Jaan tried to have someone trace them, but I guess they didn't have any luck."

"Them?" I said. "You mean you've gotten other threats like this?"

"I was about to tell you about that when Vivian came in." Anya bit her lip. "This is the fourth message since shooting started. It's like someone wants to scare me off this project."

"That's what it sounds like," I agreed.

"And that's not all," Anya said. "The morning

of the fire, someone left a photo in my dressing room."

"A photo of what?" Joe asked.

"Of me. It was a publicity still of me in my Deathstalker costume, but my face is cut out of it."

"Whoa," Joe said. "Creepy."

"I know." Anya shuddered. "Especially since it appeared while I was just a few yards away shooting a scene. That means whoever left it must've been someone with access to the set. I just can't believe . . ." She hesitated, her voice trailing off.

"What?" I prompted.

She shook her head. "Never mind. I'm just feeling a little paranoid right now. It's stupid."

"It's not stupid at all," Joe assured her. "Can we see the photo?"

She shook her head. "It burned in the fire."

Too bad. That photo might have been our best clue so far. "Do you think it's the same person doing everything?" I asked Anya. "The text messages, the photo, the fire?"

"No clue," Anya said. "But it's really freaking me out. It's going to be kind of a relief to get away from the set, even if it's just for one day."

"Get away?" I wasn't sure what she meant. "To where?"

"Didn't Jaan tell you?" Anya looked surprised.

"We're going to the FanCon in New Jersey today. It's like some huge science fiction and comics convention."

"Totally!" Joe looked excited. "I've always wanted to go to FanCon! You're going there today?"

Anya glanced at her watch. "The limos are supposed to leave in fifteen minutes. It's some kind of publicity thing for the film."

Talk about bad timing! How were we supposed to investigate if half the cast was off at some convention all day?

"Who's going to the convention?" I asked Anya.

"Most of the primary actors, plus Jaan and Stan and a few support people. The assistant director is staying here with Scorch and the rest of the crew. They're going to shoot some special effects stuff with some of the extras while we're gone."

Okay. Time to look for another silver lining. Maybe with the main actors out of the way, Joe and I could talk to the remaining cast and crew and figure out whether any of them might have reason to want Anya out of the picture.

"We should probably head over to wait for the limos," she added, checking her watch again.

We? Uh-oh. I belatedly realized she expected me to come along and play my new role as personal bodyguard—and fake boyfriend.

But maybe that was okay. "Guess we'll split up for today," I told Joe. "You can hang around here and check things out, and I'll start getting to know the rest of the cast at the convention."

"Yeah." Joe sounded disappointed. "Makes sense."

Anya glanced from me to Joe. "Oh, I was really hoping you'd both come to the convention!" she said. "Please? I have no idea when Big Bobby's going to show up, and I'd feel a lot safer with both of you there."

I hesitated. Having both of us spend the day away from the movie set—the scene of the crime—seemed like a big waste of time.

But Joe can never resist a pretty face. Besides, I knew he was dying to check out FanCon.

"Sure, that should work," he told Anya eagerly. "It'll be fun."

"We're not here to have fun," I reminded him. "Besides, how are we going to explain why some random extra gets to tag along?"

Joe shrugged. "Easy. We just need to add a few details to the story you told that lady."

"Vivian," Anya supplied. "She's Harmony's agent."

"Whatever," Joe said. "Anyway, let's say we didn't just go to camp together. Maybe I saved your life. . . . I pulled you out of the water after you got conked on the head with a canoe paddle and almost drowned."

"Hmm. It's interesting how you always end up the hero in your cover stories," I commented.

"What can I say?" Joe grinned. "The role suits me."

Anya giggled. "You two are good. I think that story will work fine. I'll text Jaan right now and let him know."

"Are we going to stand around all day waiting for Zolo?" Vance asked impatiently.

Twenty minutes had passed since we'd left Anya's dressing room. Yeah, I know Anya said the limos were supposed to leave in fifteen minutes. The trouble was, one of the actors wasn't there yet. The rest of the actors weren't too happy about it, including the blond guy we'd encountered earlier.

"Chill out, Vance," Harmony told him. "You know Zolo. He loves making an entrance."

There had to be at least two dozen people clustered around the little fleet of limos: uniformed limo drivers, several adult actors, a bunch of beefy guys who I guessed were bodyguards, and various others.

Jaan St. John was standing with Stan Redmond

and a couple of the adult actors. "I'll try calling him again," Redmond said in his brusque way. He strode off, already punching numbers into his cell.

I decided we might as well take advantage of the delay by getting to know the other teen actors. We'd already met Vance and Harmony, so I turned to a good-looking dark-haired guy.

"Hi," I said, sticking out my hand. "I'm Frank Miller, Anya's boyfriend from back home."

"Frank Miller? Seriously?" The guy shook my hand and flashed me a million-dollar grin. "Wow, I didn't even know Anya had a boyfriend. Nerd-boys everywhere will be crushed when they find out. Good to meet you, though, Frank. I'm Buzz Byers—I play Billy in the film."

Joe heard him and looked over. "You mean Susie Q's loyal but clueless boyfriend?"

Harmony giggled and sidled closer to Buzz. "That's right," she said. "Poor Billy has no idea that boys are falling all over me everywhere I go. Or even that my BFF is now Deathstalker, the venomous bringer of justice!"

"It's a good thing you're such a good girl that you'd never betray me," Buzz joked.

"So how long have you been acting?" I asked Buzz.

"Years," Buzz replied. "I made my Broadway

debut in a revival of *Oliver!* at age eleven."

"Broadway?" I echoed.

"Yeah, that's my thing. I love getting out onstage every night and feeling the audience's reactions." Buzz glanced at the movie set sprawled out behind us. "My agent talked me into giving this silver screen thing a whirl."

Joe looked at Vance. "Wait, I assumed *you* were playing Billy," he said. "So what's your role?"

"I'm Parker Oberon," Vance replied.

Joe looked confused. "Who's that? Some minor character I'm forgetting?"

"Parker doesn't appear in the comics," Harmony explained. "He's Deathstalker's love interest. They created the character for the movie because they wanted more romance."

"And because I became available," Vance put in with a smug look. "They said I was too self-confident to be believable as Billy and too young and handsome to play Dr. Brayne. So they created the role of Parker just for me."

I traded a quick look with Joe. Okay, so we were already learning some things about the cast: Harmony and Buzz seemed pretty nice and normal; Vance was totally full of himself.

Just then there was a commotion nearby. "He's here!" someone called.

"Hey," Joe said. "It's the weird-looking kid who played the alien in those old toothpaste commercials!"

Okay, so my brother isn't exactly Mr. Tactful. But he was right. As soon as I saw the guy walking toward us, I recognized him too. There was no mistaking him. He had freaky green eyes that reminded me of a snake's. They glowed out of his narrow, sepia-skinned face with its high, smooth forehead. Even though he was shorter than average, his arms and fingers were abnormally long.

"Zolo's an alien this time, too," Buzz said. "He's playing Asp."

"Oh!" Joe sounded surprised. "Okay, I can see that, I guess. But it's weird to think of Asp not being super tall like he is in the comics."

"You're not the only one who thinks so," said Buzz. "All the comics nerds have been arguing about that since casting was announced."

"That's Joe," I put in with a slight smirk. "Huge comics nerd. That's why Anya asked Jaan to let him tag along today."

"Greetings, children," Zolo said as he came slinking toward us. "Hope I didn't keep you waiting."

"You did," Vance said. "As usual."

Zolo looked unconcerned. "Patience is a virtue, my friend."

"Never mind, we're all here now." Jaan started shooing us toward the waiting limos. "Let's get this show on the road."

Joe got shuffled along toward one of the cars with Jaan, Buzz, Harmony, and Vivian, while Anya grabbed my hand and dragged me toward another. We ended up riding with Zolo, Vance, a production assistant who never took her cell phone away from her ear, and a handful of bodyguards.

"Is one of those guys Big Bobby?" I whispered to Anya as the limo wound its way through the busy city streets.

She shook her head. "He texted me again. He's going straight to the convention and will meet us there."

As I turned away from the bodyguards, I was startled to find Zolo's creepy green eyes trained on me.

"So who are you?" he asked without preamble.

"This is my boyfriend, Frank," Anya answered for me. "He flew in from Apple Valley this morning. Frank, this is Zolo Watson."

"Nice to meet you," I said.

Zolo just nodded. "You never mentioned a boyfriend before, Anya," he said in a voice so low and smooth it was practically a purr. "Keeping secrets from us, are you?"

"Of course not," she said. "It's just, I guess I never, um . . ."

"Don't let him bother you," Vance advised, glaring at Zolo. "He's just trying to get under your skin. It's his favorite pastime."

Zolo smirked and sat back against the plush leather seat. "Frank's not a bad-looking guy, eh, Bainbridge?" he said to Vance. "Hope she's not trying to sneak him in to take your place in the film. Oh wait—that's what you do."

Vance scowled. "Nice conspiracy theory, dude. Is that what your loser screenplay is about? You know, the one nobody in Hollywood wants to read?"

Zolo's green eyes went hard. "You're the last person I'm going to talk to about my screenplay, Bainbridge. So shut your trap before I shut it for you."

Vance just rolled his eyes, not seeming too worried. But Zolo turned away and hunched in the corner, looking broody and aggressive.

Hmm, interesting. Zolo's whole demeanor had changed at Vance's mention of his screenplay. What was that about?

This Zolo guy seemed pretty weird overall, actually. Was it an act? Or could there be something else going on?

Then there was his comment about replacing actors. That seemed odd too. Even suspicious, considering what had been going on with Anya.

Slipping my phone out of my pocket, I sent a quick text to HQ, asking them to send me the 411 on Zolo Watson.

SUSPECT PROFILE

Name: Zolo Watson

Hometown: Hollywood, California

Physical description: Age 17, 5'4", 110 lbs., African American. Large, piercing green eyes in a narrow face; long limbs and fingers that give him an otherworldly look.

Occupation: Actor and would-be screenwriter

Background: Zolo is the only child of an actress and a moderately successful TV producer. He's been in show business all his life, debuting in TV commercials as an infant. However, his unconventional looks have limited him to quirky bit parts.

Suspicious behavior: Has a reputation for being a weirdo in general; seems moody and unpredictable.

By the time we made it through the Lincoln
Tunnel, Zolo seemed to shake off his bad mood
and go back to normal—well, as normal as he was
before, anyway. I spent the rest of the ride listening to the actors talk about their favorite topic:
themselves.

Anya was pretty quiet, staring out the window
at the scenery alongside the New Jersey Turnpike.
But Vance and Zolo had a lot to say—to me, to
each other, to the disinterested bodyguards. When
all that failed, Vance seemed perfectly content to
talk to himself.

Most of what he said wasn't too useful. I learned
that he was dating an actress named Amy Alvaro,
that he was determined to be the most successful

actor in Hollywood by the time he turned twenty-one, and that he was pretty full of himself, as I'd already figured out.

Finally we arrived at our destination. The convention was being held at a big hotel complex that was attached to a large shopping mall. Our limo pulled up to the curb behind a couple of the others.

Anya peered out the tinted window. "Wow, there are tons of people out there," she said, sounding nervous. She looked wistfully toward the mall. "This is weird. I kind of wish I was just coming here to shop with my friends, like I used to do back home."

"Get used to it, baby. This is your life now." Vance straightened his shirt collar and ran his tongue over his front teeth. "You'll love it!"

A second later the door swung open. There was a horde of screaming fans waiting, pressed up against a velvet rope lined by uniformed security guards. Vance jumped out first. I was next in line, so I clambered out and reached back to help Anya from the car.

As she straightened up, I glanced around, checking to see if Joe was here yet.

Instead, I spotted something small and white flying out of the crowd—straight at Anya!

JOE

Fandemonium

The scene outside the hotel was wild. At least fifty people were waiting to greet us.

Well, not *all* of us. Nobody gave me a second glance as I hopped out of the limo. But as soon as Harmony appeared, people started shouting her name and her television show character's name, too.

I glanced at the next limo. Frank was helping Anya out when I saw movement from the corner of my eye. My ATAC training taught me to assess and react quickly, and it didn't let me down. I leaped forward, throwing my body between Anya and the object zipping toward her.

"Look out! Incoming!" I howled.

I felt something hit me on the shoulder. Okay, definitely not a bullet. Not even close. It felt more like a . . .

"Paper airplane?" I muttered, glancing down. Weird.

Frank had already reacted too. He dove into the crowd, grabbed the guy who'd thrown the paper plane, and took him down.

"Hey!" the guy cried, sounding surprised.

There was a moment of chaos. Jaan hustled Anya and the others toward the hotel entrance. Several bodyguards and security people waded into the crowd to help Frank. Good. It looked like that guy wasn't getting away.

I reached down and scooped up the paper airplane. It was made out of white construction paper, but it was surprisingly heavy.

Flipping it over, I saw why. There was a tiny motor attached to the bottom.

Double weird.

Frank and the guards dragged the guy forward. He was in his early twenties, tall and average-looking. But his outfit was far from average. His brown hair was slicked back, and he wore a polka-dot bow tie, flared red pants, platform boots, and a lab coat.

Then I spotted the name tag on the coat. Now I got it. The kid was dressed as Dr. Brayne.

"You don't understand!" he exclaimed breath-lessly. "I wasn't trying to cause trouble. I'm sorry if I scared anyone."

"Then why'd you throw that . . ." Frank hesi-tated, glancing at me.

"Motorized paper airplane," I finished for him. Frank blinked. "Huh?"

The fan looked pleased. "It worked really well, didn't it? I wasn't sure it would. Even though I tested the design thoroughly, I wasn't able to pre-dict certain variables, like wind shear and such. But I mostly just wanted to make sure it would go far enough for Anya to get my note. Adding a motor seemed like the only way to do it. And since I have dabbled in robotics, it was an easy matter to—"

"Hold on," Frank interrupted. "What note?"

"My message to Anya," the guy said. "I wanted her to know I support her and all. You know, before she goes inside and has to deal with the los-ers who don't approve of her casting."

Frank and I looked at each other. This guy was definitely odd.

"What do you mean?" I asked him. "Who disap-proves of Anya?"

"And why?" Frank added.

"Tons of people, for all kinds of reasons," the

guy replied earnestly. "Deathstalker fans are passionate. Some preferred different actresses for the role. There was a huge online poll about it and everything. Others have seen interviews and profiles and such and think Anya's too meek to truly embody Deathstalker." He shrugged. "But I believe in giving her a chance. That's why I wrote my note."

"I don't see a note," rumbled one of the bodyguards.

"It's the plane itself." The guy sounded proud of himself. "Look!"

I unfolded the plane. Sure enough, there were words scrawled on it.

"Yeah, it says pretty much what he just told us," I confirmed, scanning it.

The guy was babbling again, something about different philosophies of acting. I wasn't too interested. The rush of adrenaline had passed. Anya was safe. Actually, she'd never been in danger. At least not from this geeky fan.

Frank seemed to be on the same wavelength. "I think this guy is harmless," he told the guards. "Might as well let him go."

My brother and I have faced down a lot of scary situations: hardened killers out for our blood, mysterious secret societies, runaway subway trains, and even a cage full of killer tigers.

But nothing prepared us for the convention.

It was insane. People in crazy costumes were everywhere. We passed six dudes in matching Superman outfits. A bunch of amateur musicians were wandering around singing a song about time travel. A cute girl in a bikini walked by in a Darth Vader mask. A throng all dressed as robots crowded into something labeled the "signing room." A world-famous science fiction writer was perched atop a stack of his books, chatting with a teenage kid about government conspiracies. A mock swordfight among people in homemade knight outfits was in play. A woman wearing a hat shaped like a spaceship walked arm in arm with a dude dressed as a vampire.

"Wow," Frank said. "This is quite a scene."

"Yeah," I said. "I wonder where the *Deathstalker* crew went."

A passing geek in a manga T-shirt heard me and stopped. "You mean the movie people?" he asked. "I saw them heading toward the hospitality suites." He pointed toward a hallway off one side of the room.

"Thanks," Frank said.

"Live long and prosper." The guy saluted us, then wandered on.

We found the hospitality suite just in time to see Zolo coming out. "Oh," he said when he spotted us. "It's Anya's secret boyfriend and his own personal superhero."

Was it my imagination, or was there a hint of suspicion in his expression? "Are Anya and the others in there?" I asked.

Zolo nodded. "See you later. I'm going to wander around and soak up the atmosphere."

Yeah. That made sense. Zolo was just as weird as the rest of this place.

Stan poked his head out of the room just in time to hear him. "Hold on, young man," the producer said to Zolo. "You'd better stay put. We're due at the press shoot in ten minutes, then the first Q & A right after."

Zolo shrugged. "I'll meet you there."

"Wait!" Stan said.

But it was too late. Zolo had already disappeared behind a passing Chinese dragon costume worn by half a dozen giggling convention-goers.

Stan sighed. "Typical," he muttered.

"What was that all about?" I wondered as Stan ducked back inside.

"I don't know," Frank said. "But I already contacted HQ for more info on Zolo. I'm thinking he's worth putting on our suspect list."

"Really? Why?"

"There was this weird moment in the car when Vance mentioned something about Zolo writing a screenplay," Frank said. "Zolo went a little berserk. It was kind of scary."

I shrugged. "So the kid is weird; seems pretty obvious."

"I know. But worth keeping an eye on. Just in case."

We went inside. The bodyguard at the door gave us the hairy eyeball, then recognized us and waved us through. Anya was sitting on a plush sofa with Harmony while a makeup artist touched up their faces. Vivian, the grandmotherly agent we'd met that morning, was hovering nearby, keeping an eye on them.

Vance was standing by a table of food near the door, tossing pretzels into his mouth. "Hey," he greeted us. "I thought we lost you. What was up with the psycho throwing stuff at Anya?"

We quickly explained. "The guards let him go," Frank finished. "They just told him to keep away from her."

"Hmm." Vance grabbed another pretzel. "I'm surprised anyone would go out of their way to support Anya like that. I mean, it's not like anyone has seen her act in anything before."

Before we could respond, Jaan called for attention. It was time to head out for the first scheduled event.

Anya hurried over to us. "You're coming with me, right?" she said, grabbing Frank's hand.

His face went kind of red. "Um . . ."

"Sure," I said. "We'll be there. Right, lover boy?"

We all followed Jaan out of the room—and were instantly mobbed by fans. The bodyguards did their best, fending off the excited nerds and ushering us toward a different hallway.

As we neared the press photo room I spotted a familiar face in the crowd. It was him—Mechanized Paper Airplane Guy. He was shouting Anya's name and jumping up and down.

"So much for staying away from her," Frank murmured.

I started to answer. But just then the people in the Chinese dragon costume returned. It looked like they were having some kind of disagreement about steering, because the back end was going one way while the front end went the other. In the chaos, Frank got separated from the rest of us by the dragon's midsection.

"Frank?" Anya sounded anxious.

"Don't worry, he'll be back," I said, putting a protective arm around her. "And I'm here."

"Thanks, Joe," she said, pausing in the doorway of the photo shoot room to smile at me. "That makes me feel a lot—"

"Deathstalker!" someone wailed.

I turned my head just in time to see a skinny young man in an Asp mask fling himself toward Anya. "We'll never survive this world without each other!"

Cover Me

"Excuse me!" I pushed against the Chinese dragon, trying to find my way back to Joe and the others.

"Ow! Dude!" someone inside exclaimed. "Watch your hands!"

"Sorry." I took a step to the side.

Just then I heard a shriek, then someone yelled, "Deathstalker! We'll never survive this world without each other!"

Uh-oh . . .

"Sorry," I muttered again, before giving the tail end of the dragon a hard shove. I still couldn't get past it. But now I could see what was going on.

Anya's face was pale. Joe and a bodyguard were

peeling a skinny guy in a mask off her. Or trying, at least. The guy had his arms wrapped around her and was hanging on tight.

Then a teenage girl with straight brown hair stepped forward. Reaching for the scraggly ponytail sticking out from under the attacker's mask, she gave it a quick, hard pull.

"Ow!" the guy howled, letting go of Anya and grabbing at his hair.

Joe took the opening and tackled the guy, knocking him to the ground. Then he yanked off the mask.

"Good moves, bro," I whispered.

I finally got past the dragon and hurried over. But by then everything was under control. Joe had the guy pinned, and he and the guards were shouting questions at him.

Harmony and Vivian had already swooped Anya off into the press room. A couple of beefy guards were at the door, so I figured she was safe.

The brown-haired girl was standing there, watching the action. "That was quick thinking," I told her. "How'd you know that would get him off her?"

"I didn't." She shrugged. "But I know Oliver is crazy about his hair."

"So you know him?"

"Unfortunately." She shook her head. "He's a total creep. He's always trying to smooch the female stars at cons and posting obnoxious comments on the big Stalker blogs." She shot the guy a look, a flicker of amusement in her brown eyes. "People always told him it'd catch up with him someday."

Stalker blogs? I'd have to ask her more about that. I smiled. "I'm Frank."

"Janice," she said. "You a Deathstalker fan?"

"Something like that." I'd just noticed that Vance and Zolo were hovering in the doorway right behind the guards. Both were staring at Joe as he continued to interrogate Oliver.

Uh-oh. The last thing we needed was to blow our cover over something like this.

I hurried forward and grabbed Joe. "Ease up," I hissed into his ear. "I don't think this is the guy we're after. Janice says he's just some random convention creep."

Joe backed away, surrendering Oliver to the bodyguard. "Who's Janice?"

I glanced around, but Janice had disappeared. "She's the one who pulled that guy's hair to get him off Anya," I explained.

"Oh. I didn't get a good look at her." Joe shrugged. "Is Anya okay?"

"Think so. The others took her inside. She should be okay in there—I don't think this photo shoot's open to the public."

Joe looked at the throngs of fans nearby. Several guards were holding them back. "Yeah. Looks like you're right. Come on. Let's find somewhere private to talk."

That wasn't easy. The convention was packed. Who knew there were so many people who liked dressing up as aliens?

Finally we found a spot in a corner of the main room where no one would pay any attention to us. We sat down and pretended to watch a costume parade going on nearby.

"So that was exciting," I said. "And here I thought this convention was going to be boring."

Joe grinned. "I know, right? You think any of it's connected to our mission?"

"No." I shrugged. "Seems like a couple of random weirdo fans to me."

"Me too. I was kind of freaked out when I heard what that guy said to Anya before he threw himself at her. Sounded like a threat. But then I remembered it's a famous line from the comics. It's even in the trailer for the movie." Joe paused, watching as a guy dressed as an elf danced by in the parade. "Still think Zolo could be a suspect?"

"Maybe." I thought about seeing him watching us from the doorway. Him and Vance. "What about Vance? I'm wondering if we should add him to the list too."

Joe looked surprised. "You mean Mr. Hollywood? Why? I wouldn't think he'd have the mental energy to harass Anya. He spends all of it on admiring himself."

"Yeah, he seems pretty shallow," I said. "But I just remembered something weird Zolo said in the car. He said something about how Anya might be bringing me in to take over Vance's role, but how that was more Vance's style or something like that."

"What's that supposed to mean?"

"I didn't think about it much at the time. But Vance mentioned later that he's dating an actress. What if he wanted her to play Deathstalker and is holding that against Anya?"

"I guess that could be a motive. If it's true . . ." Joe looked unconvinced. "Should we ask HQ to look into it?"

I pulled out my phone. "I'll text them now."

As soon as I finished, Joe checked his watch and stood up. "We should get back," he said. "It's almost time for the Q & A session."

I nodded. Unlike the photo shoot, the Q & A

was open to the public. Anya would definitely want us there.

We headed back across the convention space. The Q & A was taking place in one of the smaller meeting rooms off the same hallway as the press room. As we reached the corner, my cell phone buzzed.

"It's HQ," I said. "That was fast."

"What'd they find on Vance?" Joe asked.

I scanned the message. "Our guess was right. His girlfriend auditioned and didn't make it. So there's his motive."

SUSPECT PROFILE

Name: Vance Bainbridge

Hometown: Los Angeles, California

Physical description: Age 19, 6'2", 190 lbs., blond hair, hazel eyes. Voted hottest teen actor three years in a row at the Big Apple Awards.

Occupation: Actor; has appeared in nine major motion pictures since making his Hollywood debut at the age of thirteen.

Just then I heard raised voices from farther down the hall. Glancing around the corner, I saw Jaan facing off against a red-haired guy who had to be twice his size.

". . . must try to understand, it's all a matter of simple psychology," Jaan was saying. "It's nothing personal."

"Nice try, St. John," the big redhead snarled. "You'll regret this. You and your precious so-called actress. Count on it!"

Then he whirled around and stalked off with his huge fists clenched at his huge sides. Joe and I hurried forward.

"Whoa," Joe said. "What was that all about?"

Jaan looked startled. "Oh! There you are," he said. "Anya was just asking for you. The Q & A starts momentarily."

"Who was that man?" I asked. "Was he threatening you?"

"What man?" Jaan smiled vaguely. "Listen, I'd better go set up for the panel. . . ."

He hurried off and disappeared through a nearby doorway. "That was weird," Joe said. "Why was he playing dumb?"

"You got me. I figured we didn't need to put him on the suspect list, since he's the only other person here who knows we're ATAC agents," I said. "But now I'm starting to—"

"Hello there, boys," a voice spoke from directly behind us.

Whirling around, I saw Zolo smirking at us. Those knowing green eyes were boring into mine.

Shooting a panicky look at Joe, I realized I'd just mentioned ATAC. How much had Zolo heard? Had we just totally blown our cover?

7

JOE

Q & A

I held my breath, not daring to meet Frank's eyes. I could practically hear Zolo's snarky voice now: *Check it out, children,* he'd sneer. *We've got a couple of secret agents in our midst.*

Instead he glanced over his shoulder. "Your girl-friend's waiting for you, amigo," he told Frank. "She won't go into the panel room until you show."

"Um, okay," Frank said. "We're coming."

"Think he heard us?" I whispered as we followed Zolo down the hall. "Or is he keeping quiet for his own weirdo reasons?"

Frank barely had time to shrug before we both got swept into the conference room where the Q & A was being held. Anya was just inside, waiting for us.

"There you are!" She grabbed Frank's arm. "I asked Jaan to bring an extra chair so you can sit by me on the panel."

Vance was standing nearby. "What?" he said. "Since when are random boyfriends and girlfriends allowed on the panel? That's weird."

"Yeah." Zolo chuckled. "Very Yoko, right?"

Vance looked confused. "Huh?"

"Never mind," Zolo said, rolling his eyes.

Meanwhile Frank gave me a helpless look. I shrugged. What could we say? It was pretty clear that Jaan would do anything Anya asked. If she wanted Frank up there with her, why fight it?

I wandered off toward the audience. Part of the front row was reserved for cast and crew. There was one seat left on the end, so I took it.

"Hi," the girl sitting beside me said. She was in the first seat outside the cast and crew area. "You with the production?"

"Sure, sort of." I was distracted by watching Frank. It didn't seem very undercover to have him up there with zillions of cameras and cell phones snapping photos of him with Anya. Pretty soon he'd be posted and dissected on every geeky fan site in the world.

But what could we do? We'd just have to roll with it.

"Cool," the girl said. "What do you do?"

I finally looked over at her. Whoa. For a science fiction nerd, she was pretty cute. Straight dark hair, intelligent brown eyes.

"Oh," I said. "Uh, I'm an extra. You know. Like an actor, but not one of the main characters."

"Yeah, I know what an extra is." She looked amused. "Actually, I wanted to try out to be an extra. But my lame parents wouldn't let me skip school."

"Bummer. So you're a Deathstalker fan, huh?" I asked.

She nodded. "A huge fan," she said. "I've been reading the comics since—"

The sudden buzz of my phone cut her off. "Sorry," I said, pulling it out and glancing at it.

It was a text from Frank: JUST SAW WHO UR TALKING 2.

I sighed. Leave it to Mr. No Fun to notice. What was the harm in getting my flirt on while I waited for the Q & A to start?

WUTZ IT 2U? I texted back quickly.

Then I tucked the phone away and turned back toward the girl. "So," I said in my suavest voice. "What were you saying?"

The next buzz came quickly. Gritting my teeth, I checked the message.

IT'S HER, he'd texted. JANICE, THE GIRL FRM B4. ASK HER ABOUT THE DS BLOGS.

Janice? Oh, right. I remembered Frank mentioning the name. She was the girl who'd helped get that crazy fan off Anya by pulling his hair. But what blogs was he talking about?

"Who keeps texting you?" The girl tried to lean closer to get a look.

I quickly stuck the phone back in my pocket again. "It's nothing," I said. "Just, uh, my stockbroker."

"Yeah, right. So don't tell me," she said.

"Listen, my name's Joe," I said. "What's yours?"

"Janice."

Okay, so far so good. "Um, do you like blogs, Janice?"

She looked a little confused. "Um, sure?" she said. "I try to keep up with the major Deathstalker ones."

"Really? Like which ones?" I had no idea why Frank wanted to know about those blogs. Maybe he had a new theory about the mission.

"Well, there's a few. But the one I check the most is Stalking Deathstalker," she said. "It's definitely the most popular one out there. In fact, the blogger's right over there."

I looked where she was pointing, and my jaw

dropped. "*That* guy?" I exclaimed. "Mr. Paper Plane?"

Janice looked confused again. "I'm talking about the guy in the Dr. Brayne costume," she said. "His name is Dalton Friedrich."

I stared. Dalton Friedrich was definitely the dude who'd launched that crazy paper airplane at Anya. He was leaning forward in his seat, staring eagerly at the panel.

I glanced that way myself, wondering if I should warn someone that he was here. Just then someone toward the back of the room yelled, "DEATHSTALKER!"

Someone else echoed the cry. Soon the entire room was chanting the name: "*DEATHSTALKER! DEATHSTALKER! DEATHSTALKER!*"

I glanced around. The room was packed—it was standing room only already, and more people were crowding in. Most of them were chanting Deathstalker's name. Janice grinned and leaned toward me.

"Stalker fans are a little impatient," she said into my ear. Then she leaned away, pumped her fist in the air, and joined the chant.

I glanced up front. Anya looked nervous as the chant got louder and rowdier. Frank looked uncomfortable sitting there beside her.

The room didn't quiet down until Jaan stood

up and raised his hands. "Thank you for coming, everyone!" he said into his microphone. "Let's get started, shall we?"

That made the chanting stop. Jaan said a few words about the movie, and then opened things up for questions.

Hands shot up all around the room. A guy sitting a few rows away caught my eye. He had nerdy glasses, greasy dark hair that hadn't seen a barber in way too long, and an intense look in his eyes.

A couple of production assistants were circulating through the room with microphones. One stuck the mic in front of Greasy McNerdboy.

"Yeah, okay," the guy said, grabbing the mic and leaning forward to glare at the panel. "This question is for Jaan St. John. I just want to know, like, what in the five galaxies possessed you to cast a wimpy nobody as Deathstalker?"

A howl of protest went up from several parts of the room. One came from Dalton the blogger.

"Crawl back under your rock, Eccleston!" he shouted. "Nobody cares what you think! Don't listen to him, Anya!"

"Whoa," I said to Janice as more fans joined in the shouting. "People get really worked up about this stuff, huh?"

"Don't pay much attention to Myles," she said. "He's a total loser spaz."

"Myles?"

She pointed at the guy with the microphone, who looked pleased with the chaos he'd started. "He considers himself a superfan," Janice said. "But if you ask me, he's just a bored rich dork from Manhattan with a bad attitude."

A production assistant passed near us, and Janice's hand went up. "Thanks for taking my question," she said when the PA handed her the mic. "Are you planning to use special effects to make Zolo Watson look taller? Because otherwise there's no way any true fan is going to buy him as Asp."

You guessed it. More yelling.

Things went on like that for a while. Who knew a movie based on a comic book could be so controversial to so many people? Before long I had the gist of the drama. A bunch of people, including Janice, thought Zolo was all wrong to play Asp because he was too short. Others were outraged by the addition of Vance's character, Parker Oberon, since he wasn't even in the comics. And of course I already knew about the whole Anya thing.

Most of the panel handled it pretty well. Vance and Zolo appeared unperturbed. Jaan looked amused by all the hubbub. Stan just looked annoyed.

Anya was the only one who seemed kind of freaked out. No surprise there. When one of the PAs came up to her holding a bouquet of flowers, she jumped in surprise.

"What's that?" she blurted out.

The microphone in front of her was live, so her words bounced out and interrupted some story Vance was telling about himself. No big loss there.

"One of the fans in the back wanted you to have these," the PA said before hurrying off.

"Oh. Um, thanks." Anya smiled uncertainly at the crowd. Then she stuck her nose into the flowers. "They smell, uh . . ."

Her voice trailed off, and she looked puzzled. Staring into the bouquet, her face went pale.

Then she dropped the flowers, jumped up, and raced out of the room without another word.

Fanning the Flames

Anya's sudden departure took me by surprise. She was out of the room before I was out of my chair. I grabbed the flowers and took off after her.

Joe was on the move too. We both caught up with Anya in the hallway.

"What was that all about?" Joe exclaimed.

I finally glanced at the flowers, which I'd grabbed on instinct. "I think I know." There was a note tucked in among the blooms, where only someone looking into the bouquet could see it.

I pulled it out. In big block letters, it read:

YOU ARE NOT DEATHSTALKER. GO BACK TO NOWHERESVILLE OR U WILL REGRET IT!

"Whoa," Joe said as he read over my shoulder.

Anya was in tears. "I thought this role was the best thing that ever happened to me," she cried. "But now I think it was the worst!"

Just then the door burst open. Jaan was the first one out, followed by the rest of the cast.

"Anya!" the director exclaimed. "What happened, my child?"

"Yeah. This better be good." Vance sounded annoyed.

Harmony rushed over and put an arm around Anya. "Zip it. Can't you see she's upset?" She glared at Vance.

"Oh yeah? Well, I'm upset too!" Vance grumbled. "I don't see why Stan decided to call off the rest of the panel just because the delicate newbie had another meltdown."

Stan emerged just in time to hear him. "What was the point in continuing?" he said with a scowl. "It was barely controlled chaos in there. Somebody *please* remind me never to do another sci-fi picture!"

He stomped off. Jaan hardly seemed to notice. "Never mind, my boy," he told Vance with a smile. "Haven't you heard the old saying? Always leave them wanting more! This shall just increase the anticipation for our second Q & A this afternoon."

Then he turned toward Anya. "There, there, my dear," he cooed. "Let's go get you something cool to drink, hmm?"

Soon we were all back in the hospitality suite. Anya was huddled on a couch in the corner. Harmony was patting her on the knee while Vivian cooed over both of them. Vance was on his cell phone in a different corner. Buzz and most of the other actors were just hanging out, doing their own thing.

Well, all except for Zolo. He'd disappeared again.

Joe and I found a private spot near the food table. "What do you think?" he asked, popping a grape into his mouth. "Think that note came from the same person as the text messages and stuff?"

"Probably." I thought about it for a second. "Or maybe not."

Joe grinned. "Way to be decisive, bro."

"No, listen," I said. "All this time we've been pretty much assuming it's someone from the cast or crew causing trouble for Anya."

"Totally." Joe nodded. "Who else could get access to her trailer like that? You saw the security on the set."

"Right. But what if at least some of the trouble is coming from another direction? Some of these

Deathstalker fans seem to get really worked up about this stuff."

"Yeah," Joe agreed, reaching for a cracker. "Like, that Janice girl thinks casting Zolo as Asp was the worst decision since the invention of homework. And she seems like one of the saner ones."

"Don't forget about the guy with the paper airplane," I said. "Or the one with the mask who threw himself at her."

Joe's eyes widened. "That reminds me," he said through a mouthful of half-chewed cracker. "Did you notice that the paper airplane geek was in the audience just now? Janice told me he writes a big Deathstalker blog. His name is Dalton."

"Really?" I hadn't noticed the guy. From up on the dais, the audience had pretty much been a blur of faces. I'd only spotted Janice because she'd been talking to Joe.

Joe was already pulling out his ATAC smartphone. "Let's check out that blog. Dalton seemed pretty harmless, but he's definitely kind of obsessive about Anya."

"Good call."

It didn't take long to find the blog, Stalking Deathstalker. It was actually pretty impressive— no basic blogware default backgrounds here. Tiny airplane motors apparently weren't Dalton's only talent; the guy definitely knew his way around a computer. The graphics were awesome, with tons of comic art and photos and even some pretty clever embedded animation. Dalton's latest entry was brief and dated early that morning:

> 6:45 a.m. Off to FanCon! Srsly psyched to see the DS movie crowd f2f, esp the lovely Anya. Will report back l8r to all my sad peeps who can't be there. Ciao, D.

"Nothing to see here, I guess," Joe said, scrolling down.

"Wait. What's that?" I'd just spotted a comment below the entry. It had a lot of exclamation points and capital letters.

"Looks like someone just added it a few minutes ago." Joe scrolled a little farther so we could read the comment. It was a spitting-mad rant about the Q & A that had just ended!

"Wow," I said as I scanned it. "Whoever wrote this has serious anger issues."

"Yeah," Joe said slowly. "And I think I might know who wrote it!" He pointed to the screen name. "Look, he calls himself MylesEcc. Remember the greasy-haired dude who asked the first obnoxious question about casting Anya?"

I shrugged. "It rings a bell."

"Janice told me his name is Myles. He's some kind of weirdo Deathstalker superfan."

"Interesting." I scanned the message again. The writer seemed furious that the Q & A had ended early and insulted that nobody on the panel had taken his question more seriously. He ended with a few more digs at Anya and her inexperience. "Think we should find out more?"

"I'll send an e-mail to HQ." Joe's thumbs were already flying over the phone's tiny keyboard. "And if we're thinking unbalanced fans might be behind some of this stuff, we might as well look into that Dalton guy while we're at it."

SUSPECT PROFILE

Name: Myles Eccleston

Hometown: New York, New York

Physical description: Age 20, 5'9", 145 lbs., brown hair, brown eyes, wears glasses

Occupation: Part-time college student

Background: Born and raised in Manhattan; has a genius-level IQ but relatively poor grades; was kicked out of several expensive private schools for unknown reasons when younger.

<u>Suspicious behavior:</u> Posts frequently on blogs about Deathstalker comics and related topics. Seems unnaturally angry that an inexperienced unknown was cast as his favorite character.

<u>Suspected of:</u> Harassing Anya with notes and text messages; possibly sneaking onto the movie set to start the fire in her dressing room.

<u>Possible motive:</u> Scaring Anya into quitting her role because he disapproves of her casting.

SUSPECT PROFILE

<u>Name:</u> Dalton Friedrich

<u>Hometown:</u> Colts Neck, New Jersey

<u>Physical description:</u> Age 23, 6'1", 195 lbs., light brown hair, blue eyes

<u>Occupation:</u> Part-time sales clerk/computer tech; writes a popular blog called Stalking Deathstalker.

<u>Background:</u> Graduated from college over a year ago, and has held several low-paying part-time jobs since then. Currently works at a computer store. Lives in his parents' basement.

<u>Suspicious behavior:</u> Obsessed with Deathstalker in general and Anya in particular.

ATAC hadn't taken long to get back to us. Joe only had time to eat three or four cookies and a hunk of cheese in the meantime.

"Okay," he said as he scanned the info. "I'm not buying the savior motive HQ suggests. Dalton just sounds like a dweeb. But this Myles character? Major red flags."

"Yeah. I wonder what he did to get kicked out of all those schools. And why it's so secret that even ATAC doesn't know about it."

Joe shook his head. "Who knows? That boarding school mission we did showed us these rich kids have their ways of keeping things quiet."

Just then I saw Anya coming toward us. She had stopped crying, but she didn't look much calmer.

"I can't believe things are so crazy," she said, her voice shaking. "I wish I'd never agreed to come to this convention. I wish I'd never agreed to play Deathstalker!"

"Don't say that," Joe said. "We're on the case

now, remember? We'll figure out who's behind it all."

She looked dubious. "I guess. But in the meantime, don't leave me alone, okay? This whole place makes me nervous."

Joe and I traded a look. Her request was going to make it tough to investigate. We wouldn't exactly be able to blend into the crowd with Deathstalker tagging along.

I knew what I had to do. "I'll stay here with her," I told Joe. "Why don't you go out and look for our newest suspects?"

He nodded. "I'll report back if I find the superfans. Or anything else interesting." Grabbing one last handful of chips, he took off for the door.

"What superfans?" Anya asked me.

"We're looking into the idea that an obsessive Deathstalker fan may be sending you all those messages," I explained.

"Really? But what about that fire? Fans aren't allowed on set."

"I know. It's just a theory right now. But we need to follow up on all the angles."

Her comment reminded me how true that was. We shouldn't get so wrapped up in this superfan idea that we forget the other possible scenario. It was the more likely one, in my opinion—that the culprit was someone from the cast or crew.

I glanced around the hospitality suite. At least part of the cast and crew was right here. Zolo was still nowhere to be seen, but there was Vance—he seemed pretty down on Anya. I hadn't even met most of the adult actors yet. I recognized a few of them, though.

My gaze stopped on the guy playing Dr. Brayne, who was standing nearby talking to Vivian and Harmony. He was a well-known character actor named Michael B. Spoon who'd appeared in dozens of films and TV shows. An unlikely suspect? Maybe. But if my time with ATAC has taught me anything, it's that unlikely suspects sometimes turn out to be the guiltiest.

I was thinking about walking over and introducing myself. But just then Anya's phone buzzed.

Uh-oh.

Sure enough, her face went pale as she looked at the screen. "What?" I asked.

She held it up wordlessly. I read the text message:

U HAVE NO FRIENDS IN NYC. GO BACK 2 MIN B4 IT'S 2 L8.

9

JOE

Where There's Smoke . . .

"**T**his is crazy," I muttered, staring around the crowded convention hall. Finding two superfans in this place was like looking for a needle in a haystack . . . or a couple of geeks in a geekstack.

I glanced at my ATAC-issue class ring. Too bad its GPS capabilities didn't extend to finding nerdy superfans. Just Frank. And I already knew exactly where he was—stapled to Anya's side.

Then a gang of roving ogres rushed past. Well, a bunch of fans dressed as them did. I stepped aside to avoid getting run down.

That put me in view of some benches in an alcove near the emergency exit. There was only one person sitting there. When I saw that person's greasy dark hair, I smiled.

Score! It was him—Myles Eccleston.

When I got closer, I saw that Myles was hunched over a fancy-looking cell phone. He didn't look up until I stopped about six inches in front of him and cleared my throat. Loudly.

"Hey," I said when he finally tore his gaze off his phone.

He looked annoyed. "I'm not interested," he snapped.

"Huh? Not interested in what?"

"In whatever you're trying to sell me." He'd already returned his attention to his phone's tiny screen. "Go try the next sucker."

"Dude, I'm not selling anything." I sat down beside him. "I heard your question in that *Deathstalker* Q & A. It sounds like you've got some strong views on the new movie."

He shoved his phone in his pocket, giving me a suspicious look. "What's it to you if I do?"

Okay, the guy wasn't exactly Mr. Friendly. But I needed to get him talking. It was time for some creative lying.

"It's just that I totally agree with you, bro," I said. "I think Anya is all wrong for the part. But it's mostly a gut feeling. I'm not even sure why I feel that way."

"How about because she's *nothing* like Deathstalker?" Myles said.

I shrugged. "I don't know. She's pretty much a dead ringer, isn't she?"

"In looks, maybe." He snorted. "But so what? When it comes to Deathstalker, attitude trumps appearance."

"I see what you mean," I said. "So why do you think they cast her?"

"Don't ask me." He rolled his eyes. "I hear that St. John guy is kind of nuts. I've seen him make the actors do all these weird acting exercises and stuff."

"Really? Where'd you see that?"

Myles shrugged. "They've been shooting in Central Park for a week or two. I live only a few blocks away."

"You mean you've been to the location?" I was careful to keep my tone casual. "I heard it's a closed set."

Myles smirked. "Nothing is truly closed if one has an open and creative mind."

Just then there was a *ping* from his pocket. He pulled out his phone and glanced at it briefly. Then he rushed away, not bothering to excuse himself.

I sat there for a second, thinking about what I'd just learned. Did it mean anything? Had Myles actually been to the set, or was he just trying to make himself sound important? He definitely seemed like the type.

Either way, he was gone now. And I had another supergeek to track down. I stood up and headed back out to the main room.

Ten minutes later I was wandering around the huckster room. That's what they called this big room where people were selling stuff. There were tons of folding tables crammed in there. They were piled with books, comics, toys, photos—you name it. If it had anything to do with science fiction or superheroes, it was for sale in there somewhere.

I found my way to the section of the room devoted to Deathstalker. There was no sign of Dalton, but I spotted another familiar face browsing some first-edition comics on one of the tables.

"Janice," I said. "Hey."

She might not be a suspect, but she seemed to know all the other Deathstalker superfans. Maybe she could help me find Dalton.

"Oh, it's you," she said when she saw me. She looked kind of cranky. "Can you believe Walter sold the Slater Scorpion?"

I had no idea what she was talking about. "Um . . ."

The guy behind the table looked up. He was in his early forties, with a full, reddish brown beard. And judging by his girth and the grease stains on his Deathstalker T-shirt, a weakness for fast-food burgers.

"Give it a rest, Janice," he complained. "It's not like I had a choice, okay? I have a business to run. Besides, it wasn't really mine to sell—I was just borrowing it. The buyer made the owner an offer he couldn't refuse, so he told me to let it go."

He strode off toward a customer at the other end of the table. I looked at Janice.

"What was that all about?" I asked. "What's the Slater Scorpion?"

"I assumed you were a Deathstalker fan, since you're working as an extra on the movie and all," she said. "How can you not know about the Scorpion?"

"I'm, uh, more of a casual fan."

She looked disdainful. "Oh. Well, the Slater Scorpion is an extremely rare and unique Deathstalker artifact. It's a large blown-glass rendering of the scorpion logo that was presented to Phillip Slater at WorldCon for his lifetime of achievement."

"Phillip Slater? You mean the creator of

Deathstalker?" I said. "I thought he died a few years back."

"He did. His estate sold the Scorpion at auction." She shrugged. "Sounds like it just got sold again."

"But why was it here in the first place?"

"Walter talked the owner into letting him display it." She gestured toward the bearded guy, who was eagerly unrolling a dusty old poster for a couple of skinny college guys. "He thought it would bring more people to his table." She frowned. "But when I got here to check it out, he told me it got sold earlier today to a private collector. I can't believe I just missed seeing it in person!"

I couldn't dredge up much sympathy. But Janice wasn't paying attention to me anymore anyway. Something in her pocket let out a beep.

"That's me." She pulled out a high-tech PDA and checked it out. "There's a new post on SD." Shooting me a look, she added, "That'd be Stalking Deathstalker, for you casual fans."

"Thanks for the translation. So does that mean Dalton just posted another entry?"

"Uh-huh. I receive alerts anytime one of the major DS bloggers updates."

"Can I see?" I asked Janice.

"Sure, in a sec." She peered at the screen. "Whoa! Is it true? Does Anya seriously want to meet Dalton?"

"Huh?"

She shoved the phone into my hand. "Check it out."

I scanned the blog entry. It was dated today, just minutes ago.

> BIG NEWS!!!!!!! Just got a PM thru the site. Guess who from? ANYA HERSELF! She saw me in the crowd at the panel earlier & wants 2 meet me b/c she could tell I'm her biggest fan. I always knew she was smrt!!! Off 2 my mtg w/her on the roof right now . . . SOOO PSYCHED!!!! More l8r!!!!!

"Wow," I said. "Dude really likes exclamation points."

"Yeah. If this is for real, it's like his dream come true." Janice shrugged. "He's probably making it all up, though. Or maybe it's someone messing with him. You know—it could be someone pretending to be Anya and sending him that message to get him all excited. He'll probably get to the roof and find some fat sweaty guy dressed up in a Deathstalker catsuit waiting for him." She smirked. "It should be fun to see that on YouTube later."

I glanced at the entry again. Janice's explanation was reasonable. But something about this didn't feel right.

"Yeah, that's probably it," I said. "Look, I just remembered something. Gotta go."

All my ATAC instincts were tingling. Outside the huckster room I glanced around, looking for stairs. I needed to find my way to the roof.

I headed out into the main hall. There was a staircase at the far end, spiraling around in a big glass atrium. But I'd only taken a few steps in that direction when I heard the shrill scream of a fire alarm.

Uh-oh. What now?

I spun around and saw a couple of things. One was Frank and Anya. They'd just emerged from the hallway by the hospitality suite, along with some bodyguards and several other cast members.

The second thing I saw? Thick black smoke pouring out of a different hallway.

"What's going on?" Frank cried, sprinting toward me.

"Wait!" Anya dashed after him.

I was already running. The wail of the alarm made it hard to think.

As I ran through the hallway, I saw the source of the smoke. In one of the rooms, a life-size cardboard cutout of Anya as Deathstalker was going up in flames!

FRANK

10

Ups and Downs

I skidded to a stop behind Joe. The smoke was so thick I could hardly breathe.

"We've got to stop the fire from spreading!" Joe cried.

Glancing around, I saw a fire extinguisher on the wall. I broke the glass, whipped out the extinguisher, and threw it to Joe. He leaped into action and started spraying the flames.

The rest of the *Deathstalker* group was starting to catch up. We'd been on our way to this very room. The cast was supposed to be autographing posters and comics in there.

"Whoa!" Buzz shouted. "Stand back, everyone!"

91

Within seconds, the fire was out. "Nothing to see here, folks," a bodyguard said, shooing away some curious fans. "The fire department will be here soon. Let's leave them room to work."

"I guess this means the signing's canceled." Vance peered into the smoky room behind what was left of the cardboard cutout.

"Nonsense," Jaan said briskly, whipping out his phone. "Just give me a moment, children." He wandered off with the phone pressed to his ear.

I glanced at Anya. She looked totally freaked out. No wonder. It's not every day you see yourself burn to the ground.

"You okay?" I asked her.

"What do you think?" She was trembling. "This is insane! I'm not sure how much more I can take!"

Harmony and Vivian had been huddling near the back of the group, but now they stepped forward. "It's okay, Anya," Harmony said softly.

"Yes, it is." Vivian sounded sterner. "If you're going to be in this business, Anya, you need to realize that it's unpredictable. People aren't always going to like you, and sometimes they'll show that in extreme ways." She looked at the charred remains of the cutout. "Like this."

Anya sniffled. "But—"

"But nothing," Vivian said. "When you're in

the public eye, it's just part of the deal. So if you really want to be a movie star, you need to put up with it."

I winced. Vivian's pep talk seemed a little harsh to me. Even Harmony looked kind of surprised.

But Anya had been listening quietly. Finally she nodded.

"You're right, Vivian. Thanks," she said, straightening up. After one last, brief glimpse at the burned cutout, she turned away. "I'll be ready to do the signing as soon as someone touches up my makeup."

"Good for you!" Harmony gave her a squeeze. "Come on, I'll go back to the room with you to fix your face."

Jaan reappeared just in time to hear her. "Hurry up," he said. "The organizers are setting up another room for us. The signing will start in ten minutes."

"I'll be ready," Anya promised. "Let's go, Harmony."

She seemed to have forgotten about me, so I grabbed Joe's arm. "We should find somewhere to talk," I said.

Soon we were back out in the main room. We found a private spot behind a huge model of a spaceship.

"That's two fires involving Anya," I said. "Coincidence?"

"Doubtful." Joe shrugged. "Guess it's a good thing we both came to the convention after all."

"Yeah. Seems like whoever's after her is right here." I chewed my lower lip thoughtfully. "Trouble is, we still don't know if it's a fan or someone from the cast and crew. Did you track down those superfans?"

"Sort of," Joe said. "That reminds me—we need to get to the roof."

"Huh?"

He was already on the move. "I'll explain on the way."

As we hurried across the room toward the stairway atrium, he told me what he'd read on the blog. It didn't make much sense.

"Anya didn't send Dalton any messages," I said. "I would've seen her do it."

"Duh." Joe shot me a look. "*She* may not have contacted him, but *someone* did. Who would want to lure him to the roof of this place, and why?"

"Who cares? We're here to figure out who's harassing Anya, not what practical jokes a bunch of science fiction geeks are playing on each other."

"But this could be connected to Anya," Joe insisted. "Whoever contacted Dalton used her as bait. What if that person is trying to set her up somehow?"

I didn't answer. We'd just reached the atrium. The stairs spiraled up in the middle. The floor-to-ceiling windows on the far side looked out over a big fountain court between the hotel and the mall.

"What's going on out there?" I said.

A couple dozen people were out in the courtyard. Most were definitely from the convention. You could tell by the costumes and T-shirts. Almost all of them were staring upward.

Joe tossed an impatient glance out there. "Who knows," he said. "Maybe someone's trying to launch the Starship *Enterprise* off the . . ." His voice trailed off, and he looked outside again.

"Off the roof?" I finished for him. "Come on. Let's see what's going on."

We rushed outside and looked up. Everyone was staring at the roof of the two-story restaurant behind the fountain that connected the hotel to one end of the mall.

"Whoa!" Joe said. "It's Dalton!"

Dalton was up on the roof, leaning over the safety railing. The railing was about three feet high and set back a few inches from the smooth concrete drop-off.

"What's he doing?" I said.

"Climbing over that railing," Joe said grimly. "Is he nuts? That ledge is way too narrow to walk on."

More people were still pouring out into the courtyard. One of them was Janice. She spotted us and hurried over.

"What's going on out here?" she asked. Then she looked up and gasped. "Oh, wow! What's *that* doing up there?"

For a second I thought she meant Dalton. Then I followed her gaze. I'd been so busy looking at Dalton that I hadn't noticed the plank sticking out from the edge of the roof like a weird little diving board. It was a few yards to the left of where Dalton was. The glass skylight of the restaurant was raised up in that area, which meant you couldn't reach the spot from which the plank extended without edging along the narrow roof edge.

The plank stuck straight out over the courtyard, jutting out approximately three feet. It was hard to see how it was attached to the roof. But it was easy to see that something was sitting on the other end—a chunk of glass about the size and shape of a shoe. It looked like some kind of statue.

Joe saw it too. "What's that?"

"Are you blind? It's the Scorpion!" Janice exclaimed. "The Slater Scorpion!"

"The what?" I said.

"Whoa, seriously?" Joe said to Janice. Then he turned to me. "It's some kind of rare Deathstalker doodad. It was supposed to be on display here at the convention, but a collector bought it earlier today."

I had no idea how he knew all that. This didn't seem like the time to ask. Dalton was sliding carefully down the wrong side of the railing.

"Did Dalton put that scorpion thing there?" I asked, still not really understanding any of this.

"Maybe," Janice said. "This could be a stunt to publicize his blog or something. He's done nuttier things in the past."

Yeah. That I could believe. Especially when I thought back to that motorized paper airplane.

"Dalton, stop!" Joe called up to him. "It's too risky. Let us help you get down from there, okay?"

Dalton glanced down. Even that small movement made him sway dangerously. His foot almost slipped off the edge of the roof, but he caught himself on the railing.

"There's no time!" he called, sounding hysterical. "The countdown is already down to ten seconds!"

He took another wobbly, precarious step toward the plank. A few people in the crowd gasped. Others whooped and hollered.

"What countdown? What's he talking about?" Joe said.

I was peering up at the board sticking out over the courtyard. "Hey," I said. "There's something on the other end. Can you see it?"

"It looks like a clock," Janice said, squinting. "That's weird."

"Five seconds!" Dalton howled, lurching forward another step. He was almost within arm's reach of the plank now.

Joe and I exchanged a look. Suddenly this was all making sense. Okay, a really weird kind of sense. But still.

"Countdown," Joe said.

"Timer," I added. "That board must be set to drop that glass thing when it hits zero."

"No way!" Janice cried. "But the Scorpion . . ."

The sudden clang of an alarm cut her off. The crowd gasped as the plank shuddered and dropped an inch or two. The glass scorpion slipped toward the edge.

"Nooooo!" Dalton howled.

He let go of the railing and lunged forward, grabbing for the glass scorpion. His fingers came within inches of it.

But at that moment the board came loose.

The Scorpion tumbled off the board, plummeting down and shattering on the hard stone tiles of the courtyard two stories below.

A split second later, Dalton fell to the ground right beside it.

11

JOE

Plans of Action

A few minutes later, we watched the paramedics do their thing. They'd already strapped Dalton to a stretcher and given him a shot of something to stop the pain. Now they were loading him into the ambulance parked at the edge of the courtyard.

"It looks like they've got him stabilized," Frank commented.

Janice was still standing near us. "Do you think he'll be okay?"

"Yeah. He's really lucky." I watched the ambulance pull away.

Frank and I had moved in immediately after the fall. First, of course, we'd checked on Dalton. He was only semiconscious. There was a bone sticking out of one leg while the other leg was twisted under him at an odd angle. But fortunately, he was alive.

A woman dressed up as some kind of alien had pushed forward through the crowd, saying she was a nurse. We'd stepped back and let her take a look at Dalton. At least half a dozen people had already dialed 911, so that was covered.

Next we'd gone over to check out the Slater Scorpion. Or what was left of it. Several fans were eagerly scooping up bits of the shattered glass. To keep as souvenirs, I guess.

Once the ambulance was gone, the cops got to work. A couple of officers started cordoning off the scene while others began questioning bystanders.

"Let's get out of here," I whispered to Frank. "There are plenty of witnesses to tell the cops what happened, and we have other things to do."

Janice had already headed over to grab her own piece of the Scorpion. Nobody was paying any attention to us as we headed inside.

"Wow, this place cleared out," I commented when I got a look at the main hall. When we'd been in there last, the room had been packed. Now there were only a few dozen people wandering around.

"Yeah," Frank agreed. "Some of the crowd's still out in the courtyard, of course. Others are probably at that signing event. Who knows where the rest went."

"Maybe they've been called back to the mother ship."

Frank rolled his eyes. "Hey, did you get a load of that timer setup?" he asked as we stopped near a deserted book display.

"Yeah. Hard to tell with it smashed to bits, but I'm guessing the alarm clock was wired to that spring. When the alarm went off, the spring released the plank and the glass scorpion went smasho." I shook my head. "I still don't get it, though. Who set it up?"

"Janice seemed to think it was Dalton himself," Frank said. "Maybe this really was some bizarre publicity stunt gone wrong."

I thought about that. "That theory makes a weird kind of sense," I agreed. "These Deathstalker fans are all about the superhero thing, right? He could've been setting himself up to save the Scorpion."

"Only he messed up the timing and then lost his balance." Frank nodded. "Seems possible. We already know he's good with gadgets."

"There's just one problem," I said. "How'd

he get his hands on that glass scorpion? The way Janice was talking, it sounds like it would've cost a bundle to buy it."

"And according to ATAC, Dalton doesn't have a lot of money and lives in his parents' basement." Frank bit his lip. "Yeah, that part doesn't really make sense. I wish we knew whether Dalton really got a private message from someone pretending to be Anya."

"Think the ATAC hackers could find out?"

"Maybe, given some time. But we need answers sooner than that. We don't even know if the whole Dalton disaster is connected with the mission we're supposed to be working on."

He had a point. "So what do we do next?"

Frank checked his watch. "The cast signing should've just ended, but they're supposed to head straight back to the media room for some radio interviews or something."

"Okay," I said. "So let's use that time to talk to more Deathstalker fans. Maybe we can figure out whether Dalton's the type to have set up the Scorpion thing himself."

"Works for me." Frank headed toward the schedule board posted in the middle of the room. "Let's see where we're likely to find some."

Soon we were scanning the schedule of events.

"Looks like the only Deathstalker event going on right now is a LARPing thing over in one of the ballrooms," I said.

"LARPing?" Frank looked confused.

"Live-action role play," I said. "That's when people dress up and act out their roles as fantasy characters and stuff."

"Oh. You mean like historical re-enactments of the Battle of Gettysburg?" Frank asked.

Yes, leave it to my brother to make a nerdy activity sound even nerdier. "Something like that, I guess. Come on, it's supposed to be starting right now. Let's go check it out."

When we entered the ballroom, it looked like the world's weirdest bar mitzvah. A few dozen people were milling around, all of them in costume. I spotted three or four Dr. Braynes, half a dozen Asps, and a Susie Q or three. Most of the rest were miscellaneous aliens.

Near the door, five different people dressed as Deathstalker were facing off. "I get to go first!" one girl insisted. "Dalton promised!"

"Dalton's not here, remember?" The second Deathstalker was actually a guy. At least I was pretty sure. It was hard to tell under the long brown wig and heavy makeup. "And Harold said I could go first!"

A few yards away, a bunch of people in Asp or other alien masks were grabbing cardboard swords out of a box. "Check it out—grozzers!" I said, recognizing the distinctive double-bladed shape from the Deathstalker comics.

"What's a grozzer?" Frank asked.

"Alien weapon," I told him.

There was no time for further explanation. A whine of feedback directed everyone's attention to a nervous-looking kid holding a microphone. "Hello, fellow Deathstalker fans," the kid squeaked out. "Welcome to our ninth annual FanCon gathering. I'm sorry to report that our usual game master, Dalton Friedrich, won't be able to make it this year."

There were lots of nods and exchanged glances among the costumed LARPers. It looked as if almost everyone had heard about Dalton's fall.

"Anyway, I'll be stepping in," the kid continued. "I know Dalton would never want us to break tradition. So let the battle begin!"

"Okay, maybe this is a waste of time," Frank murmured as the kid started calling out instructions to the players. "Nobody's going to want to talk to us during this."

I nodded. "Maybe you're right. We should probably go see how Anya's holding up. I wonder if she heard what happened to Dalton yet."

"Hope not." Frank grimaced. "That could be all it takes to send her over the edge . . . so to speak."

We stopped talking as a loud cheer went up from the LARPers. The game was starting. One of the costumed Deathstalkers stood in the middle of the room. An alien took a swing at her with its grozzer, but she repelled the attack with a kick of her leather boot and then did an awkward somersault toward the next alien. That alien landed a blow on her shoulder with its grozzer before she grabbed the fake weapon and tossed it away.

I was ready to move on. Yeah, I liked the Deathstalker comics and all. But who wanted to spend their time whacking each other with cardboard swords?

"Come on," I told Frank. "Let's get out of here."

As I turned away, I saw a third alien jump at Deathstalker with its grozzer raised. It landed a blow on her arm.

This time the costumed Deathstalker didn't fight back. She staggered backward with a shriek.

"Hey!" she cried, grabbing her arm. "I'm bleeding!"

For a second I thought this was all part of the game. Then I remembered. In the comics,

Deathstalker bleeds bluish green—like those scars on her body. And the substance I could already see seeping out from beneath the girl's hand was red.

Blood red.

FRANK

12

The Razor's Edge

Seconds after the girl screamed, Joe started babbling. Something about green blood.

I couldn't hear him too well. Shouts and screams were coming from all over the room. Meanwhile the person in the alien costume who'd landed the blow ripped off her Asp mask.

It was Janice!

"No way!" she cried, staring at the other girl, her face white with shock. "I'm so sorry—I don't know what happened. . . ."

I rushed over with Joe at my heels. While I checked the injured girl's arm—luckily, it seemed to be only a flesh wound—Joe grabbed the sword out of Janice's hand.

"Check it out," he said after a quick look. "Someone taped a bunch of razor blades along one edge!"

"Whoa." I looked at Janice. "What's the deal?"

"I don't know." She looked more shaken than ever. "I just grabbed one out of the box like everyone else!"

"Really?" I must have sounded skeptical, because she frowned.

"Yes, really," she said. "What, do you think I'm a psycho?"

Nearby, I heard the game master babbling into his cell phone for help. Joe was staring at Janice.

"You have to admit this looks pretty strange," he told her. "Where'd those fake swords come from, anyway?"

She shrugged. "I don't know. I guess Dalton brought them."

Someone had dropped one of the cardboard swords on the floor nearby. I picked it up and took a look.

"No razor blades on this one," I said.

Joe grabbed a sword out of the hand of the nearest costumed alien. "Hey!" the guy behind the mask complained.

"None on this one either," Joe reported, ignoring the alien. "Looks like you might have the only grozzer in the place that can actually draw blood."

Janice crossed her arms over her chest. "So what are you saying? You think I sliced that girl on purpose? Because if you think that, you're crazy."

Joe and I traded a look. Was there anyone who wasn't crazy in this place? I had to wonder.

Before we could continue, several security guards burst in. After finding out what had happened, a couple of guards took the injured girl to get first aid and others dragged Janice and the game master off for further questioning.

"That was freaky," Joe said once they were gone. "Think she did it?"

I shrugged, glancing around the room. Most of the LARPers were standing around in small groups, talking about what had just happened. A few were swinging at each other again with their fake swords.

"She does seem to be around a lot when strange things are happening," I said. "And we know she feels strongly about Deathstalker."

"But not about Anya." Joe shrugged. "She's all about the tall/short Asp debate."

"Whatever. Can't hurt to get some more info on her, right?" I pulled out my phone to text HQ.

SUSPECT PROFILE

Name: Janice Lang

Hometown: Merrick, New York

Physical description: Age 17, 5'6", 140 lbs., brown hair, gray eyes

Occupation: High school student and Deathstalker superfan

Background: Straight-A student from a stable family. In addition to her strong interest in Deathstalker, Janice's hobbies include Web design and playing the clarinet.

Suspicious behavior: Has been present or nearby during most of the convention incidents. Wielded fake sword that injured someone. Is upset with the casting of Zolo Watson as Asp.

Suspected of: Harassing Anya at FanCon.

Possible Motive: Unknown; possibly trying to sabotage entire production?

We spent the next few minutes questioning the other LARPers. It soon became obvious that most of them knew one another. And almost everyone knew Janice. Apparently she was a serious super-fan. They all knew Dalton, too.

"Yeah," a guy in a Dr. Brayne costume said when I asked him about Stalking Deathstalker. "Everyone reads it. It's the best DS blog out there. That's why everyone's so upset that Dalton got hurt." He hesitated. "Well, almost everyone."

Almost everyone? I was about to ask what he meant by that. But just then I heard a sudden shriek.

I spun around. A guy in an alien mask was holding up his hand. Blood was dripping from a shallow gash in his palm.

Joe was nearby talking to a cute girl dressed as Susie Q. He leaped toward the bleeding guy.

"What happened?" he asked. "Did you grab Janice's sword?"

"No, I just got this one out of the box!" the guy exclaimed, clutching his injured hand.

I hurried over and grabbed the sword the guy had just dropped. "More razors!" I reported grimly.

"So it wasn't just Janice's," Joe said. "Let's check out the rest."

We investigated and found two more swords with razor blades taped to them. The others were okay.

"Scary," Joe said, staring at one of the razor swords. "Anyone could've sliced and diced someone without realizing it."

"Good thing nobody got hit in the face with one of those," I said. "But what does this mean?"

He thought hard, then shrugged. "It probably means Janice is innocent."

"Then who did this? And why? Who's the target?"

"Got me," Joe said. "I don't see how it could have anything to do with Anya, though."

Before I could respond, my phone buzzed. It was Jaan.

"Is Anya with you two?" he asked.

"No," I replied. "Isn't she with you? I thought you guys were doing that radio interview."

"Anya left once she finished her part," Jaan said. "I thought she returned to the hospitality suite. But she's not here, and she's not answering her phone. It seems she has disappeared!"

13

JOE

Malled

"**W**e're on our way," Frank said into his phone. "On our way where?" I followed as he headed for the door.

"Anya's missing," Frank said tersely. "Jaan doesn't know where she is and can't reach her by phone."

"Whoa!" I groaned. "You mean we lost the person we're supposed to be protecting?"

Frank didn't answer. He just sped ahead. Seconds later we burst into the hospitality suite.

Jaan was waiting for us. We dragged him off to a private corner near the door. Urgent or not, we couldn't risk being overheard. There were lots of other people in the room: Vance was picking at the food table; Michael B. Spoon was chatting with the other adult actors and a couple of PAs; Buzz was playing a video game.

"What happened?" Frank asked.

Jaan looked vaguely worried. "I don't know. Maybe nothing. Harmony isn't here either—perhaps they're visiting the ladies' room. You know how girls are about that sort of thing, eh?"

Under the circumstances, I wasn't ready to be quite so optimistic, especially since Vivian wasn't there either. It seemed a lot more likely that Harmony had gone somewhere with her.

"So nobody's seen her since she left that interview?" I asked Jaan.

"Seen who?"

I spun around. "Dude!" I exclaimed when I found Zolo's freaky green eyes gazing at us. From, like, two feet away. How did he *do* that?

Frank cleared his throat nervously. "Um, we were just trying to figure out where Anya went."

"Didn't she tell you?" Zolo smirked. "I thought you were supposed to be the boyfriend."

Was he onto us? I still couldn't tell.

"Do you know where she is, my boy?" Jaan asked Zolo.

"Sure." Zolo slouched against the wall nearby. "She and Harmony went to the mall."

"They what?" Frank said.

Zolo shrugged. "Said they wanted to get away from the craziness for a while. They were going to sneak off to the mall, do some shopping. You know—girl stuff."

"Oh, dear," Jaan said. "I'm not sure that was such a grand idea."

I saw his point. Anya seemed awfully fragile right now. And Harmony was pretty famous because of her old show. If they got mobbed by fans, things could get ugly.

"We'll find them," Frank said, already heading for the door. "Come on, Joe."

"What's the matter?" Buzz asked, stepping forward. "Are Anya and Harmony okay?"

"I'm sure they're fine," Jaan assured him. "They're just having some girlish fun over at the mall, and we don't want them overrun by eager fans. Not to worry, though. These boys are off to track them down and bring them safely home."

Buzz nodded. "Yeah, Anya's already pretty weirded out by all the attention she's been getting today. The last thing she needs is a bunch of *Young Hearts* fans squealing and knocking her over to get to Harm," he said. "Want me to come along and help find them?"

"Um, that's okay," I said quickly. "I mean, you

probably have another event coming up or whatever. Wouldn't want you to miss it."

"Nope, there's nothing on my schedule for the next hour."

"Okay," Frank said. "But we're sort of trying to stay under the radar. What if you get recognized?"

Buzz chuckled. "Probably not a problem. I'm pretty well known in Broadway circles. But nobody in New Jersey goes to the theater. I'm all yours!"

I shot Frank a look. What now? There was no easy way to turn down his offer to help. Not without blowing our cover. Besides, time was ticking. The more time Anya and Harmony spent over at the mall, the more likely they'd be recognized.

Besides, what was the big deal? This just meant Frank and I couldn't discuss the case while we looked for Anya. It wasn't as if we were making much progress anyway.

"Sure," I said. "The more the merrier."

"How are we ever going to find them here?" Frank asked.

The three of us were wandering down the mall aisle. It was crowded with weekend shoppers:

kids traveling in packs, parents pushing strollers, old people ambling along at the speed of a stalled turtle.

"No clue," I said, dodging a pack of giggling tweens sipping on slushies.

"We just need to think like a couple of teenage girls," Buzz said. "It's like an acting exercise!"

"Okay, you're the actor, right?" I said. "So where are they?"

Buzz looked thoughtful for a second. Then he shrugged. "Okay, I give up," he said. "I'm not *that* good an actor."

"Maybe they're in a shoe store." Frank paused, staring into the nearest storefront. "Girls like shopping for shoes, right?"

Yeah, we were pretty hopeless. And the mall was huge—two stories, probably two hundred stores. We could have wandered around all day and never found them.

But just then we heard a commotion. Shouts. Squeals. Excitement.

"Sounds like something's happening upstairs." I hurried toward the nearest escalator.

"Think it's them?" Buzz asked as he and Frank followed.

"Let's find out," Frank said.

When we reached the top of the escalator, for a

second I still couldn't move. That was because a crowd was gathered in the aisle nearby.

"Excuse me. Pardon me," I said, pushing my way through.

"Harmony!" a young woman shrieked into my ear. At about five zillion decibels. My entire head vibrated from the sound.

But at least I knew we were on the right track. "Come on," I called over my shoulder to Frank and Buzz. "I think they're here."

We fought our way to the center of the crowd. That's where we found Harmony and Anya. They were backed up against a display of bath salts outside a makeup store. A mall security guard was doing his best to keep the crowd at bay. But it was a losing battle.

Most of the shouting seemed to be for Harmony. I guess Anya wasn't famous outside geeky circles yet. Still, she looked pretty freaked out as she stared at the hysterical fans.

Harmony saw us first. She nudged Anya and pointed, then waved at us. The security guard helped usher us through to them.

"Wow," Harmony exclaimed when we got there. "Am I glad to see you guys!"

Anya just nodded, her eyes wide and nervous.

"Same here." I pulled out my phone. "I'd better

call Jaan and let him know you're okay."

Harmony looked puzzled. "What do you mean? Didn't Stan tell him where we went? Vivian was going to ask him to let everyone know."

"Stan?" Frank glanced at me. "I didn't even see him in the room, did you?"

I shrugged. What difference did it make? "The important thing is we found you," I said.

"Sorry if we worried anyone," Anya said. "We didn't mean to cause trouble."

"It's okay." Buzz glanced around. "But we'd better get you back before these fans start a riot."

Anya nodded. "It's kind of scary, isn't it?" she said softly. "I'm just glad they're paying more attention to Harmony than to me. I'm not sure I'm ready for this sort of thing."

"Don't worry, you get used to it," Harmony told her.

Anya didn't look too convinced.

More security guards had finally arrived to help. They were holding the crowd back. Still, tons of people were screaming Harmony's name and jumping up and down, trying to get her attention.

Then I heard a male voice shout Anya's name. Anya heard it too. Her head whipped around, trying to see who'd said it.

A second later a huge slushy cup came flying straight at her.

"Look out!" Frank shouted.

Too late. The cup hit Anya in the forehead, slopping icy blue slushy drink all over her!

FRANK

14

Booking It

I spotted someone racing away. "There!" I yelled. "It was him!"

Not waiting for a response, I took off. I heard Joe's shouts for Buzz to stay with the girls, then his footsteps pounding after me.

I kept my eyes on the guy I was chasing. He was average-size, wore ordinary sneakers and jeans, but the rest of him, including his head, was covered by a dark gray hoodie.

"Stop!" I yelled.

He didn't stop. He didn't even look back. He just dodged through the crowd of shoppers.

"Sorry," I said breathlessly as I pushed myself through the people.

Just ahead, I saw the guy vault over a bench and skid around a corner. Joe and I followed.

Now we were in another arm of the mall. This one had a wider aisle. In addition to the stores on either side, there were a bunch of kiosks all down the center.

"Great," Joe panted in my ear. "Obstacle course."

"Go left," I told him.

Joe nodded and peeled off, sprinting along the left side of the row of kiosks. I stayed to the right. That way, Hoodie Guy couldn't duck into a store to hide without one of us seeing him.

He was still running. I saw him swerve around a kiosk crammed with stuffed animals, only he slipped and crashed into it. Fluffy kittens, ducks, and unicorns went flying everywhere.

"Hey!" the girl working there cried. She glared at me as I reached the kiosk. "Stop!"

"Sorry," I called as I raced past. I almost tripped on a stuffed puppy, but caught myself just in time.

That cost me a few seconds, though. When I looked up, the guy was disappearing around another corner.

Joe and I got there at the same time. "That way!" Joe blurted out, pointing.

The guy was just leaping over the edge of a railing. Onto the escalator below.

We followed. An old guy with a cane stepped out in front of us, heading toward the escalator.

"Look out!" Joe cried, throwing himself aside just in time.

"Oh, dear!" the old man said disapprovingly.

"Come on!" I yelled to Joe. "If we lose sight of him before he gets downstairs, we'll never find him!"

We reached the down escalator at the same moment as a huge group of little kids. It looked like some kind of birthday party, with lots of little girls in pink hats.

"Oh, no!" I moaned as they all poured onto the steps ahead of us. There was no way we could push our way through that mob. Not without causing some serious pink mayhem.

But Joe didn't slow down. "Follow me!" he called over his shoulder.

Vaulting over an especially slow-moving kid, he jumped—right onto the escalator's handrail!

"Whoa!" he exclaimed. He teetered from side to side, his sneakers squeaking on the rubbery, moving handrail. For a second I thought he was going to fall. If he went one way, he'd crash down to the floor below. If he fell the other way, he'd take out half the birthday party. A couple of little girls screamed. So did at least one of the adults with them.

Then Joe found his balance. He started moving, half running and half sliding down the steep handrail.

I shrugged. If he could do it . . .

"Aaaaaah!" I cried as I leaped onto the handrail. I tried not to look down. Let Joe call me an Eagle Scout if he wants—there was no way I'd squish those kids. If I lost my balance, I was going to throw myself the other way.

But I kept my balance. Scooting down that narrow railing wasn't easy. It was sort of like surfing on the world's narrowest board . . . or skateboarding after losing two or three wheels. I got as far as I could, and then jumped the rest of the way.

I landed hard right beside Joe. He was already looking around.

"There he is!" he cried.

I spotted Hoodie Guy too. He was darting into a large sporting goods store. Maybe we could trap him in there.

"Let's go!" I yelled.

Joe and I raced into the store. It was one of those big, echocy places. Shelves and bins full of balls, bats, nets, sneakers, and all kinds of other sports equipment filled the aisles.

Hoodie Guy was still in view near the front. He was right next to a huge bin stuffed full of dozens—possibly hundreds—of multicolored tennis balls.

He looked back at us, but his hood still covered his face. "Stop!" I yelled.

Hoodie Guy did stop—just long enough to shove his shoulder into the bin of balls. It tipped, sending a rainbow of tennis balls bouncing right at us! "Aaaah!" Joe cried, fending off the balls.

I did the same, ignoring the yells of the store's employees and customers. Through the rain of balls, I saw our target dart back out of the store entrance. "He's getting away!" I cried. "Come on!"

We ran, tripping over the balls rolling everywhere. By the time we hit the mall aisle, Hoodie Guy was twenty yards away and moving fast.

"Hurry!" Joe called. "It looks like he's heading for the food court!"

We actually made up some ground as we raced along the aisle. Whoever this guy was, he was no sprinter.

Then he hit the food court. The first food stand was a pizza place. Half a dozen tempting-looking pies were set out on the counter. Hoodie Guy paused and grabbed one—a large pepperoni, by the looks of it.

"Hey!" the pizza guy yelled.

Hoodie Guy ignored him. He turned and flung

the pizza, sending it flying right at us like a big, cheesy Frisbee.

It was easy to dodge it. But it cost us another second or two. That gave the guy time to race ahead into the main part of the food court. It was a big, round area with food stalls around the outside and tables crammed into every inch of space in the middle. The tables were packed. Lots of people had set shopping bags beside their chairs too. There was no easy path through.

The guy we were chasing seemed to realize it too. He jumped onto a table—and started jumping from one to the next! Wails of anger and dismay rose from all around. Guess he was taking out a lot of lunches along the way.

"Think someone will grab him?" Joe panted as we skidded to a stop.

"We can't count on it." I glanced around. "He can't go very fast that way, anyhow. Let's go around."

Joe nodded. We each went a different direction, taking the aisle between food shops and tables.

It was a gamble. Hoodie Guy was taking the shortcut straight across the circular area. Going around the outside was a lot longer. I pushed myself as fast as I could, hoping to cut him off. Halfway around, I glanced in to see how far he'd gotten.

"No!" I shouted.

Hoodie Guy had turned around—and was heading back the way he'd come!

"Joe!" I screamed at the top of my lungs. "He's going back!"

I had no idea if he heard me. Probably not. It was pretty noisy in there, with people talking, food-making equipment clanging and steaming, and of course the Muzak pouring out of the mall speakers.

Spinning around, I sprinted back toward the food court entrance. I got there just in time to see Hoodie Guy racing away.

"He went back!" Joe called from somewhere behind me.

"I know!" Not waiting for him, I took off. Thirty yards ahead, Hoodie Guy spun around another corner.

I raced around too—just in time to see him duck into a storefront. It was a bookstore. There were racks of sale books across part of the front, leaving only a narrow entrance.

I smiled. This was our chance! We had him trapped.

"Is he in there?" Joe asked breathlessly, skidding to a stop beside me.

"Yeah. Stay here and guard the entrance so

there's no way he can slip out. I'm going in!"

"Wait!" Joe said.

But I didn't. I hurried inside.

The bookstore was kind of claustrophobic. The register and some tables filled the front part. The back section was filled with tall shelves packed with books forming narrow aisles. The place was like a maze.

I stayed low as I crept along the front, peering down each aisle. If the guy burst out and tried to push his way past me, I'd be ready.

I didn't see him, so I picked an aisle at random. Maybe he was hiding out in back, or keeping just ahead of me, dodging from one aisle to the next. Whatever. He couldn't get away as long as Joe was guarding the entrance.

Creeping slowly down the aisle, I held my breath and listened for footsteps.

I was almost at the next cross path when I heard a weird noise from the next aisle. It was sort of a scraping sound accompanied by heavy breathing.

"Hey!" I called. "Who's there?"

The noise came again. *Screeee . . .*

That was when I noticed the bookcase above me moving. It was starting to topple. Books slid out and were crashing down as the huge bookcase fell straight toward me!

JOE

A Shocking Development

"I'm going in!" Frank yelled.

"Wait!" I said.

But he ignored me. Nice. He dodged through the maze of tables piled high with books, disappearing behind a stack of dictionaries. Who even uses those anymore?

I thought about following him inside. But I knew that would be stupid. As long as one of us was at the entrance, Hoodie Guy couldn't get away. We had him trapped. All we had to do was flush him out, and he was ours.

I just wished it was Frank doing the guarding, and me doing the nabbing.

The woman behind the counter was staring at

me. She looked suspicious. I smiled innocently, then pretended to look at some books on a nearby table.

But I was so impatient I couldn't focus. Why was taking Frank so long?

Then I heard someone call my name. But it wasn't from inside the store—it was from the aisle outside.

Buzz was hurrying toward me, with Anya and Harmony right behind him.

At least I guessed it was Anya and Harmony. Both girls were wearing enormous dark glasses and floppy straw hats. Anya had also wrapped a weird shawl around her entire torso and practically half her legs. Probably to hide the slushy stains.

"Nice disguises," I said when they reached me. "Very inconspicuous."

Buzz grinned. "Did you catch the guy who threw the slushy at Anya?"

"Working on it." I shot a look into the store. Still no sign of Frank. "Do me a favor, okay? Hang here and make sure he doesn't leave. He's wearing a dark hoodie."

"Okay, sure," Buzz said, looking kind of confused.

Harmony had lowered her dark glasses. She was staring at me.

"What are you, some kind of real-life superhero?" she asked. "I thought you were just an extra."

"Oh, that's Joe for you," Anya said with an awkward little laugh. "My boyfriend Frank says they used to play superhero at camp all the time. . . ."

I didn't stick around to hear any more. With luck, we wouldn't need our cover stories much longer anyway. At least if Hoodie Guy, whoever he was, turned out to be the one causing all the trouble.

I dove into the store, looking for Frank and our target. Jogging past the first few aisles, I didn't see either of them.

Suddenly I remembered my class ring gadget. I glanced at it. Should I use it to locate Frank?

Then I caught movement just inside the next aisle. I stepped over, thinking it might be Frank or the other guy.

But it wasn't. It was a girl. A really, really cute girl around my age. Sort of bookish, but in a hot way. She'd just pulled a book off the shelf.

"Hi," she said when she saw me looking.

"Hey." I returned her smile. "What are you reading?"

Before she could answer, I heard a sound: sort of a scraping, and then some grunting. It was coming from a couple of aisles down.

Oops. I suddenly remembered where I was and what I was supposed to be doing.

"Uh, excuse me," I told the girl, taking off.

I followed the sounds to the right aisle. When I glanced in, I saw him. Mr. Hoodie! He was bent over what looked like a broom handle wedged against the bottom edge of one of the bookcases. He grunted, and the broom handle squeaked against the floor.

The tall bookcase swayed a little. He was obviously trying to use the broom as a lever to tip it over. Why? I didn't think too much about that at first. I was too psyched—I had him! There was no way he could outrun me from this close.

I was about to dive down the aisle after him. Then . . .

Creak!

The bookcase tipped a little farther. I heard books slide off and crash down in the next aisle.

That was when I realized what he must be doing. "No!" I shouted.

The guy glanced over. I still couldn't see his face in the shadow of the hood. But I wasn't really looking anymore either. I'd already seen that it was too late. The force of gravity was taking over—that bookcase was going down.

I leaped toward the next aisle and dashed around

the corner. Frank was standing at the far end. He was staring at the tipping bookcase, frozen in place.

"Frank!" I yelled. Then I sprinted down and flung myself at him.

"Oof!" He grunted as I tackled him hard. We both flew out the end of the aisle and hit the ground in the cross aisle.

A half second later, there was a loud crash as the bookcase fell. Books scattered everywhere. The bookcase hit the next one in line, making it sway a little. But it stayed upright. Whew!

"Whoa," Frank said, pushing himself to stand. "That was close. Thanks, bro."

"Anytime, bro." I heard the sounds of voices as people hurried toward us. Soon we were surrounded.

"Are you okay, you guys?" Buzz asked anxiously.

Uh-oh. As soon as I saw him—along with Harmony and Anya—leaning over us, I realized what it meant. In all the commotion of the bookcase collapse, everyone had come running. That meant nobody was guarding the store entrance.

We'd lost Mr. Hoodie.

"All's well that ends well, as they say." Jaan shook his head. "But perhaps it might be prudent if we packed up and headed back to the city a little early, hmm?"

It was a few minutes after the bookstore incident. Frank and I were back at the convention along with the others. Anya had apologized for scaring everyone, insisting it was all her fault.

Now Jaan seemed ready to call it quits on the whole FanCon thing. I couldn't say I blamed him. I was already trying to figure out a cover story so that Frank and I could stay behind and keep investigating, when Vance spoke up.

"No way!" he said, sounding annoyed. "I'm supposed to be part of another panel this afternoon. It's the one called 'Old Worlds, New Faces'—it's about new characters brought in to add excitement to existing franchises. From what I hear, it's going to be *very* popular. Why should I have to miss it?"

"He has a point, Jaan," Michael B. Spoon said. "I was kind of looking forward to judging this afternoon's costume parade myself."

A few others nodded or murmured their agreement. Anya looked uncomfortable.

"It's okay, Jaan," she said softly. "I don't mind if we stay. I can just hang out here in the hospitality suite while you guys finish up."

Jaan shrugged. "Well, if you're sure . . ."

"Come on," Frank whispered, giving me a tug on the arm.

We slipped out into the empty hallway. I grinned.

"Trying to escape before Anya remembers you're supposed to be her bodyguard?"

"Something like that," Frank admitted. "We don't have any time to waste sitting around. Not if we're going to figure out what's going on."

"I hear you. So what's our next move?"

"I'm not sure. I really wish we'd caught that hoodie guy." He sighed. "Think there's any chance he was one of our suspects?"

"Well, he definitely wasn't Vance," I said. "He's way too tall to be Hoodie Guy, and it sounds like he was hanging out in the hospitality suite the whole time we were at the mall. And I'd say Dalton's out too. I'm guessing he won't be running like that for a while."

"Right." Frank grimaced. "What about that other kid, what was his name? Myles? Or Janice, or even Zolo?"

"Guess it could've been any of them. Although I was pretty sure Hoodie Guy was, well, a *guy*." I thought for a second. "Think it could've been Janice who yelled Anya's name right before that slushy came flying?"

"Maybe, if she disguised her voice." Frank shrugged.

Just then the door to the hospitality suite flew

open. The cast and crew started pouring out. Anya was with them.

"There he is," she said, hurrying over to Frank. "Jaan talked me into doing the next panel. I said I'd try, but only if you could sit with me again."

"Oh." Frank swallowed hard. "Um, okay."

He looked at me. I shrugged. What could we do?

I thought about slipping away to investigate on my own. But I decided against it. Trouble seemed to follow Anya wherever she went. If she was leaving the safety of the hospitality suite, maybe it was better if we both kept her in sight.

The panel was another Q & A, the afternoon session of the earlier one. There was already a crowd gathered inside. Jaan hurried in, along with Vance, Buzz, and most of the others.

Anya paused just outside, staring through the doorway. "Coming?" Harmony asked.

"In a second," Anya said, her voice shaking. "Go ahead."

Harmony looked uncertain. Then she shrugged and hurried into the room.

"You okay?" Frank asked Anya.

She shook her head. "I thought I could do this," she said. "But I don't think I can. It's too much."

Frank shot me a helpless look. He really has no

clue when it comes to dealing with girls. I stepped closer.

"You'll be fine, Anya," I said soothingly. "Seriously."

She looked unconvinced. "I don't know," she mumbled. "How many people are in there?"

I stepped to the doorway and looked into the room. Yeah, just as I'd thought. It was packed.

The cast and crew were milling around behind the panel table. Jaan had already taken his seat in the middle. A few others were still finding their places.

I looked the other way and scanned the audience, wondering if Mr. Hoodie was out there, waiting for another shot at Anya. It was a creepy thought.

Then I spotted two familiar faces. Janice was slumped down in her chair, and Myles, who was slouched up against the wall with his hands shoved into the pockets of his jeans. He looked kind of unhappy.

Frank called. He was still back in the hallway with Anya.

And no wonder. Dalton's accident had probably put a damper on things, especially since most of these Deathstalker fans seemed to know one another.

I glanced at the panel again. Jaan was looking over at the door with a troubled expression. "Is Anya coming?" he called to me.

"She'll be right in," I replied.

"All right." Jaan still seemed concerned. He leaned forward to speak into the microphone sitting on the table in front of him. "Please bear with us, people," he said. "We must delay this little gathering until someone very special arrives to take the chair to my right." He waved a hand at the empty seat next to him.

"Is that all we're waiting for?" Vance sounded impatient. He jumped up from his place a couple of chairs down, flung himself into Anya's seat, and reached for her microphone. "Then there's no need to wait. I'm ready to start answering questions right—"

BZZZZZT!

As Vance's hand touched the mic, he suddenly jerked violently in place. Sparks flew, and a split second later the room went black.

Blackout

Anya screamed as the hallway lights—along with every other light in view—went out.

"Hey!" I yelled. "What's happening?"

I wasn't the only one yelling. Screams and shouts were coming from everywhere. It sounded as if the whole convention had lost power. Maybe even the entire hotel.

"Frank?" Anya said, her voice quavering. "Where are you?"

"Right here. It's okay." I groped around until I found her hand. "I have an emergency flashlight on my key chain. Just let me find it. . . ."

The tiny beam wasn't very strong, but it was enough for me to find my way over to the doorway.

"We've got to get to Vance," Joe said as soon as I got there. "I think he got electrocuted by one of the microphones!"

"Oh no!" Anya moaned.

"Anya?" a voice called. "Is that you?"

It was Stan. He was standing just inside the room with the crew members who weren't on the panel. Whew! I steered Anya over to him.

"Can you keep an eye on her?" I asked.

"Uh, sure, I guess," Stan said uncertainly. But Anya seemed okay with it. In fact, she collapsed into the producer's arms, sobbing.

Joe and I didn't stick around to watch. The room was in chaos—the bodyguards were doing their best to keep everyone calm, but it wasn't really working.

Using my light, we made our way to the panel table. Jaan and some of the others were bending over Vance, who was slumped on the table. He was moaning, which under the circumstances seemed like a good sign.

"How is he?" Joe asked.

Vance lifted his head. "I'm okay," he rasped. "But I feel like I got struck by lightning."

"I think the shock was enough to give him a strong, painful zap," Buzz said. "But fortunately, the surge blew out the power before it could really injure him." At my surprised look, he shrugged. "My dad's an electrical engineer."

"Please remain calm, everyone!" Jaan called out. "Everything is under control!"

Okay, that was pretty much a lie. Things seemed to be escalating—there was no way that electric shock was an accident. But who'd done it and why? We were running out of time to figure it out.

"Let's get out of here," Joe hissed.

"Okay," I said. "Follow me."

I kept the tiny flashlight on until we were almost to the door. Then I flipped it off. I didn't want Anya to see us leaving and try to come with us. She was safe enough with Stan, and we could work faster without her tagging along.

Working by feel, we made our way out of the room and a few steps down the hall. "You there, bro?" Joe whispered.

"Yeah, I'm here." I kept the light in my hand but didn't turn it on. Better not to attract attention. People were already running in and out of the room. Some were using their own cell phones for light. But they were all heading away from us toward the main hall.

"So what do you think?" Joe said.

"I don't know. Why would someone electrocute Vance?"

"I don't think they were going for Vance," Joe replied. "I'm pretty sure the mic he grabbed was meant for Anya."

"Whoa," I said. "Okay, that makes more sense. So which of our suspects could've rigged it?"

"I don't know. But Buzz sounded like he knew a lot about electricity," Joe said. "You don't think we should add him to the list, do you?"

"He couldn't have been Hoodie Guy," I pointed out.

"True. Okay, then what about our superfans?" Joe said. "Think they could do something like this?"

"Maybe. They're both techie types, right?" I said. "And they were both right there in the room."

"Yeah. Think ATAC HQ found out why Myles got kicked out of all those schools yet?"

Before I could answer, someone else spoke out of the darkness. "Oh man, it's so obvious!" Janice's distinctive voice said. "It has to be Myles doing all this crazy stuff!"

I gasped and flicked on the flashlight. Janice was standing there in front of us.

"And hey," she added, "are you guys really with ATAC? I didn't even think that was real!"

JOE

In the Dark

"Janice!" Frank blurted out, sounding panicky as he shone his light in her face.

I knew how he felt. Our cover was as blown as the power. Now what?

"Where did you come from?" I demanded. "We didn't hear you coming!"

"Obviously." She rolled her eyes. "Honestly, that's making it kind of hard for me to believe that you two are some kind of supersecret teen agents."

"Whatever," I muttered.

"Anyway," she said, sounding excited, "did you say you think Myles might've set up that microphone to zap Anya? Because that totally makes sense!"

"It does?" Frank said.

"Yeah. He's an angry guy. I'm already pretty sure he's the one who set up Dalton."

"Wait, what?" I peered at her in the dim light of Frank's light. "What do you mean? You think Myles rigged up that Scorpion thing?"

"Uh-huh. Dalton and Myles were big rivals." She snorted. "At least Myles thought so. I'm not sure how seriously Dalton took any of it; he kind of seemed to enjoy it all."

"What kind of rivals?" Frank asked.

"Didn't you read any of Dalton's blog?" she said. "Myles was always sniping at him on there and on some of the other DS sites too. He and Dalton were always trying to humiliate each other."

"So you think Myles was trying to humiliate Dalton by making him fall off the roof?" It sounded a little far-fetched to me.

"I doubt he intended for him to fall," Janice said. "Myles is crazy, but maybe not *that* crazy. He just knew it would drive Dalton nuts to have to stand by helplessly and watch the Slater Scorpion shatter. He probably never guessed Dalton would climb out and try to save it!"

"Yeah." I shuddered, remembering the way Dalton had dived right off the roof.

"Anyway, who else would be nuts enough or

have enough free time to set up something like that?" Janice said. "Not to mention enough money to buy the Scorpion just to destroy it."

"So Myles has a lot of money?" Frank asked.

"His family's loaded," Janice said matter-of-factly. "They live in some fancy-schmancy building right on Central Park West." She shrugged. "Didn't you know that already? I thought you were supposed to be professional spies."

"Um . . ." Frank sounded troubled. I knew it had to be driving him crazy that our cover was blown. That was, like, rule numero uno for ATAC—stay undercover. And Frank is a rules-following kind of guy.

But I figured it wasn't worth worrying about now. Janice knew the truth. We might as well go with it.

"Do you think it's possible Myles could have been targeting Dalton *and* Anya?" I asked her. "Because we're really trying to figure out who's been sending Anya threats and stuff."

"Oh, totally," Janice said. "You heard him at this morning's Q & A. Myles has been ranting nonstop ever since they announced the casting. He has a huge crush on this one actress from his favorite science fiction TV show that got canceled last year, and I guess he convinced himself she was the only one who could truly embody Deathstalker." She shook her head. "Nuts, right?"

Considering her own strong opinions about the Asp casting, I decided not to comment. "Myles claims he visited the set in New York," I reminded Frank. "Think he could've set that fire and planted that photo?"

"Maybe," Frank said. "It's definitely worth talking to him."

We hurried back to the panel room. At least half the occupants were gone. The rest were mostly milling around, bumping into each other in the darkness, waiting for information on what was happening.

"It's not going to be easy to find Myles in this mess," Frank murmured.

"He was here before, right?" I said. "Turn on your light and let's see if he's still around."

I led him and Janice over to the spot where Myles had been standing. There was no sign of him. I was looking around the rest of the room when Jaan hurried over.

"There you are, boys!" he said, not even noticing Janice. "Is Anya with you?"

"What?" I had a familiar sinking feeling. "No. Isn't she with you?"

"We left her with Stan," Frank put in.

Stan appeared behind Jaan. "She ran off after you two disappeared," the producer said with a frown. "I tried to stop her, but she ignored me." He shook his head. "Actresses! They'll be the death of me, I swear. . . ."

"Oh man, not again!" I said.

Frank sighed. "I'll look for her," he said. "You two see if you can find Myles."

"Let's just hope we *don't* find them together," I said.

"True," Janice said. "But hold on—I have an idea."

She flipped her phone around so the screen was facing her. Then she started typing on the tiny keyboard.

"What are you doing?" I asked.

"Posting a comment on Stalking Deathstalker," she said, still typing. "I'm asking anyone who's here at the con to keep an eye out for Myles and post where he is if they see him."

"Oh." I was skeptical. Who was going to be checking in on some blog in the middle of a blackout?

But Janice had hardly finished when her phone alert buzzed. It was someone posting to say they'd seen Myles less than five minutes ago!

"Says he was in the main hall," Janice reported. "Heading north-northwest."

I tossed Frank a wave, then hurried off with Janice beside me. It took us a few minutes to find our way to the main hall in the dark. In that time, more posts popped up on the blog. One claimed to have spotted Myles on the fifth moon of Uranus, and another said he'd been seen running naked through the mall. But the rest actually seemed to be for real.

"It sounds like he was heading toward the ballroom," Janice said, scanning the latest one. "Should we go see if he's there?"

"Definitely."

When we got there, the ballroom appeared to be empty. I peered in through the door. No sign of the craziness from outside.

"False lead," I said. "Where else could he have gone?"

Janice shook her head, shining her PDA light around. "I bet he's hiding out in here," she whispered. "For all his bluster, he's a total coward. It would be just like him to lay low until the lights come back on."

I realized this was the same ballroom where we'd witnessed the LARPing incident earlier. Still, I wasn't convinced that made it any more likely that Myles would hide out here. But why not check it out? It was just as likely we'd find him here as stumbling around in the dark outside.

"Okay, let's take a look," I said.

Janice nodded, then turned off her light. "Stay quiet so he doesn't know we're coming," she whispered. "I assume as a trained agent you know how to do that, right?"

I rolled my eyes, even though she couldn't see me in the dark. "Let's go," I whispered back.

We crept across the room toward the far wall. That was where I'd seen the boxes of props and costumes and such stacked earlier. Maybe Janice was right; maybe Myles was hiding out behind the boxes.

We were halfway there when the sudden buzz of my cell phone made me jump. Beside me, Janice let out a squeak of surprise.

I grabbed the phone, hitting the mute button. But I was afraid it was too late. If Myles was in here, he'd know someone was coming.

We stood still for a second, listening. Then Janice grabbed my arm and gave it a tug, indicating we should keep going. I peered around as we tip-toed forward, willing my eyes to adjust. But it was way too dark to see much beyond vague shadows.

After a few more steps, I realized Janice wasn't

within arm's reach anymore. "Where are you?" I whispered as softly as I could. "Janice?"

BZZZZZT!

I gasped as the lights suddenly blazed back to life. After so long in the dark, the glare was blinding.

"There he is!" Janice shouted. "Joe, look out!"

"Huh?" I started to turn. But I stopped when I felt the cold, hard steel of a blade pressed against my throat.

"Don't move," Myles hissed in my ear.

FRANK

18

The New Normal

After Joe and Janice left, I tried calling Anya. Her phone went straight to voice mail, so I started searching. I had no idea where she'd gone. I decided to go with the logical approach. Using my flashlight, I worked my way down the hall.

I found her less than ten minutes later. She was leaning against the wall, talking on her phone. When she saw me, she hung up.

"Are you okay?" I asked.

"How's Vance?" she asked without answering my question.

"He'll live. The electricity didn't have time to build to a dangerous level before it cut off," I told her. "At least that's what Buzz said. Anyway, Vance should be fine."

Anya nodded. "Good. I don't want anyone else to get hurt because of me. I almost decided to leave for real this time when I realized what had happened."

I wasn't sure what to say. I suddenly wished Joe was there. Okay, so he's nowhere near the girl magnet he thinks he is. But at least he's comfortable talking to them. I had no idea what to say to make Anya feel better.

Then I noticed that she actually looked calmer than before. "*Almost* decided to leave?" I echoed.

"Yeah. I even called Vivian to ask if she could help me book me a flight back to Minnesota tonight." She shrugged. "She does that stuff for Harmony all the time. Plus, I knew if I asked Jaan, he'd try to change my mind."

"So what did Vivian say?"

Anya played with the phone in her hand. "She said everything was up to me. She reminded me that I'm the one in control of my life and that I'm not really Deathstalker. I'm not trapped by circumstances and forced to become a creature I barely recognize. I'm free to walk away anytime, to go back to my happy hometown life and forget all about being a movie star . . . if that's what I want."

"Uh, so is it?" I asked uncertainly.

She smiled. "No," she said. "Hearing her say that made me realize I really *do* want to be an actress. That's why I let my friends talk me into going to that audition. It's why I've been working so hard to get better and learn everything I can. I want to be Deathstalker—I know I can do it. I'm not going to let some creep ruin it for me. Or hurt my friends, either!"

"Um, okay." She was actually sounding kind of empowered all of a sudden. Jaan would be thrilled to hear that Vivian's little pep talk had worked.

But I had other things on my mind. Like Joe. Had he and Janice found Myles yet?

"Listen, let's get you back to Jaan and the others," I said. "Joe and I think we may have figured out who's behind all the trouble. Joe's trying to find him right now."

"Really? Who is it?" Anya exclaimed.

"One of the Deathstalker superfans," I said. "His name is Myles. He asked the first question at the morning Q & A session."

"I remember him. He seemed really intense."

"That's putting it mildly. We found out he may have visited the movie set in Manhattan. And he's got a history of overreacting to Deathstalker-related stuff." I shrugged. "Plus, well, you heard him at the

Q & A. He's not crazy about your casting."

"Oh." For a second she looked upset. Then she squared her shoulders. "I want to come with you to find him."

Huh? I definitely wasn't expecting *that* reaction!

"I'm not sure that's a good idea," I said. "He's acting kind of erratically, and we don't know what he'll do once he knows we're onto him."

"I want to see him." Anya sounded determined. "If he's the one who's been trying to scare me, I want to face him. I want to show him that I'm not scared anymore."

Wow. It was as if she was transforming into Deathstalker right in front of me. Kind of impressive, considering how she'd been before. That must have been one heck of a pep talk.

I still didn't think it was the best idea to let her tag along. But I didn't have time to talk her out of it either.

"Okay," I said. "But be careful and follow my lead, okay?"

She nodded. "Got it."

I sent a quick text to Jaan, letting him know that Anya was with me. Then I called Joe to find out where he was.

He didn't answer. That was weird.

"What?" Anya asked, seeing my face.

"Nothing. Just trying to figure out where my brother went." Suddenly remembering that class ring gadget, I flipped open the top. "This should lead us to him."

I peered at the readout. It was a little hard to decipher. The gadget was new to me, and I hadn't had a chance to practice with it yet.

"I think he's this way," I said at last. "Come on."

We headed down the hall and out into the main room. The lights were still off, and people were running around in the dark.

"This is creepy," Anya said as a group of ogres rushed past us.

"Look on the bright side," I said with a wry smile. "At least you won't get recognized."

She actually laughed. "True," she agreed.

I smiled. Score! Maybe I wasn't so hopeless at talking to girls after all. All I needed was a blackout and a tense situation to do it.

We continued on, following the gadget's readout. I checked our position every few yards. The ring pointed us across the way and down another hall. I realized we were heading for the ballroom where Janice had sliced up that other girl.

"Where are we?" Anya asked as I stopped in front of the ballroom door. "Is he in there?"

"Myles? I don't know," I said. "All this thing tells us is where my brother—"

BZZZZZT!

I squeezed my eyes shut, blinded by the sudden glare as the power returned. Ragged cheers erupted from the direction of the main room.

But I hardly heard them. Another yell had just met my ears from inside the ballroom: *"Joe, look out!"*

My eyes flew open. "That was Janice!" I exclaimed.

I rushed forward, bursting into the room. Almost immediately, I skidded to a stop.

"Joe!" I shouted.

He was at the other end of the room. Myles was behind him, holding one of those alien sword things to his throat. It had to be one of the ones with the razor blades attached.

"Frank!" Janice cried. She was standing about ten feet from Joe and Myles. "Do something!"

"Stop right there!" Myles yelled as I took a few steps forward. He sounded on the verge of hysteria. "Don't come any closer, I mean it!"

"Take it easy." I came to a stop and raised both hands in front of me. "Let's not do anything crazy, okay? We just want to know why you're causing all this trouble."

Myles's eyes were wide and panicky. He looked like a cornered animal.

"I didn't mean to hurt anyone," he cried. "Not really. I never thought Dalton would end up jumping off the roof like that. It wasn't my fault!"

"So you set up that Scorpion booby trap?" Joe asked.

I had to hand it to him. He sounded pretty calm for a guy with a knife to his throat.

"Well, yeah," Myles said. "But I never thought he'd jump! I was just trying to take him down a peg, you know? I wanted to show him he's not the high and mighty king of all Deathstalker fans just because of his stupid blog. He had to see that he doesn't control everything."

"So you really did destroy the Slater Scorpion over your petty, stupid, pathetic little rivalry?" Janice spoke up, sounding disgusted. "Some fan you are!"

"Whatever." Myles glanced at her. "You wouldn't understand."

That was true. We didn't. But that was the least of my worries right now. I needed to figure out a way to get Joe to safety and then capture Myles before he could hurt anyone else.

Before I could come up with anything, Anya stepped past me. I'd almost forgotten she was there.

"You're right, Myles," she said in a clear, strong voice. "I don't understand."

Myles goggled at her. I guess he hadn't noticed her standing back in the shadows by the door.

"A-Anya?" he blurted out.

"That's right." Anya took another step toward him. "I hear you think I'm a terrible Deathstalker. So why don't you come say it to my face?"

That seemed to confuse him. As he gaped at her, the arm holding the sword slipped slightly.

That was all the opening Joe needed. "Hi-ya!" he shouted, grabbing the arm and twisting it so that Myles dropped the sword.

"Hey!" Myles blurted out.

I was already sprinting forward to help. But Joe didn't need it. By the time I got there, he had Myles on the ground.

"Nice work, bro," I said.

"Thanks," Joe replied breathlessly. "Good call to have Anya distract him like that."

I didn't bother to tell him it wasn't my idea. "Go find a security guard," I told Janice. "We need to get this guy into custody."

Ten minutes later, several guards were dragging Myles away to wait for the police. Joe, Anya, Janice, and I watched until they were gone.

"Wow," Janice said. "That was pretty cool. Now

I really do believe you guys are secret agents!"

"Yeah," I said. "I just wish we could've convinced Myles to confess to everything."

While waiting for the guards, Joe and I had questioned him some more. Quite a bit more, actually. He'd admitted to planting the swords to try to get Dalton in trouble. He confessed to writing the note in the flowers in that morning's Q & A and to being the slushy-throwing hoodie guy. And of course he had no hesitation about owning up to his various online rantings when Janice brought that up. He actually seemed proud of those.

But when we mentioned the two fires—the one in Anya's trailer and today's poster burning—he claimed to have no idea what we were talking about. It was the same with the texted threats, the vandalized photo from Anya's trailer, and the electrified microphone.

"Don't stress, dude," Joe advised me. "The cops will get him to spill his guts about that other stuff."

Anya nodded. "Maybe he realized he was in big trouble and decided to clam up before he made things worse for himself. Anyway, I'm just glad things can go back to normal now."

I bit my lip, still feeling troubled. But I didn't say anything. For one thing, I didn't want to ruin Anya's happy, empowered mood.

"Back to normal," Anya echoed thoughtfully as we all headed toward the door. "I guess maybe my life won't ever be totally normal. Not the way it used to be. But maybe that's okay. There are different kinds of normal, right?"

"Sure," Janice said.

We stepped out into the hallway. Now that the lights were back on, the convention seemed to be going back to normal too. Lots of people were still milling around.

One of them, a skinny guy in his twenties dressed as a zombie, stopped to stare at Anya. "Deathstalker!" he blurted out. "Oh, wow! I'm your biggest fan!"

"Thanks." Anya smiled at him. "I really appreciate that."

"Cool," the guy said. "So, like, can I have one of your eyelashes for my collection?"

Anya's jaw dropped. "Um . . ."

Janice scowled. "Beat it, you freak!" she said, shooing the guy away.

I traded a look with Joe. Normal? Yeah, maybe that was pushing it.

19

JOE

Loose Ends

"**O**kay, that's another mission tied up in a day. Are we the world's most awesome ATAC agents or what?" I leaned back in my chair and grinned at Frank.

We were sitting in Jaan's office back on the movie set. The limos had dropped us off a few minutes ago. It had been a long day at the convention, but now it was over.

"So, how about that beach idea?" I added. "We've still got plenty of time before we have to be home."

Frank didn't answer. I'm not sure he even heard me. The dude had been totally distracted since we'd captured Myles. Right now he was staring fixedly at that stuffed croc on Jaan's wall.

"Frank?" I said. "Earth to Frank!"

"Huh?" Frank finally snapped out of it. Sort of. "What did you say?"

"Nothing. Just that I think real aliens are landing right outside this trailer. They're probably planning to take us all back to their home planet and eat our spleens for dinner."

"Oh . . . Listen, Joe," Frank said. "I can't stop thinking about how Myles reacted when we asked him about the fires and stuff. What if he really didn't do all that?"

Typical Frank. He always had to dot every *i* and cross every *t*. "Leave that to the cops, dude," I said. "They'll figure it out."

"But if it wasn't Myles . . ." Frank shrugged. "I'm just wondering if maybe we should stick around here for another day or two. Just in case."

I grinned. "Hey, if you want to hang out and watch the pretty girls, just admit it, bro!"

"It's not that." Frank frowned at me. "I just—"

He stopped talking as the door opened. Jaan walked in with Anya.

"Thanks for waiting, my boys," the director said. He pulled over another chair for Anya, then sat down himself. "I thought we should talk. What do you call it in your business, eh? A debriefing?"

"Sure," I said. "I guess."

"Did the police get Myles to confess?" Frank asked.

"In a manner of speaking, yes. He told them that he had two purposes to his mischief at the convention," Jaan said. "To make that other fellow look foolish—"

"You mean Dalton," Frank said.

Jaan nodded. "—and to express his displeasure with our lovely Anya, and I suppose with me for casting her. Apparently he had another note waiting in the wings for me at the second Q & A, telling me I was a blight on the face of the movie industry and no better than a blind monkey with a camera. From what I understand, he even drew a picture to go along with it." He shrugged. "Sadly, the police said the note was vital evidence and wouldn't let me have it. I was planning to frame it for my collection."

Anya giggled. "Oh, Jaan!"

I chuckled. That did sound like something Jaan would do. At least based on seeing the rest of his office.

Frank didn't even crack a smile. "So did he own up to the other stuff?" he asked. "The fires, the texts, the microphone?"

Jaan hesitated. "Not yet," he said. "He still

insists he knows nothing about those matters. The police are still working on it, though."

"Hold on." Anya sat up straight, looking nervous. "Myles didn't confess to the fire in my trailer? Or cutting up that photo?"

"Well, not in so many words," Jaan said. "But—"

The buzz of a cell phone cut him off. We all automatically reached for our phones. But it was Anya's.

I saw her face go pale as she looked at the screen. Uh-oh.

"What is it?" Frank asked, suddenly on alert. "Another text?"

She nodded wordlessly and held it out for all of us to see.

U WILL NEVER B DEATHSTALKER! GO HOME
B4 EVERYTHING U CARE ABOUT GOES UP IN
FLAMES—JUST LIKE WHAT HAPPENED 2 HER!

"Oh, dear," Jaan whispered.

Frank glanced at me. "I think we're going to have to postpone that beach trip a little longer."

"Yeah," I said with a sigh. "I guess we are."

FRANKLIN W. DIXON

THE HARDY BOYS

Undercover Brothers®

INVESTIGATE THESE TWO ADVENTUROUS MYSTERY TRILOGIES WITH AGENTS FRANK AND JOE HARDY!

#28 Galaxy X

#29 X-plosion

#31 Killer Mission

#32 Private Killer

#30 The X-Factor

#33 Killer Connections

From Aladdin
Published by Simon & Schuster

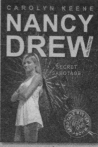

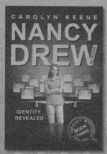
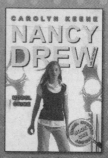

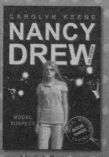